Buckingham Pet Palace may provide services fit for a four-legged king, but there's no use crying over spilled kibble—not unless it leads to murder!

When a break-in at the Pet Palace robs Sue Patrick of more than her beauty sleep, she intends to tidy her ransacked doggy daycare and spa before making any rash decisions. But after Sue abandons her better instincts to rescue a petrified pug stranded at a lighthouse in the Delaware Bay later that morning, she's lured off mainland Lewes long enough for a freshly murdered body to get dumped in her driveway . . .

Aided by Lady Anthea Fitzwalter, her practically royal business partner from across the pond, Sue sniffs out clues about the yappy pug with a complicated history and the old car spotted at both crime scenes in hopes of IDing the culprit. As the investigation leads them back to the bay, the ladies soon find themselves immersed in a case trickier than a canine agility course—and chasing after a well-groomed killer who will do anything to maintain a perfect reputation . . .

Visit us at www.kensingtonbooks.com

Books by Lane Stone

Pet Palace Mysteries
Stay Calm and Collie On
Support Your Local Pug

Published by Kensington Publishing Corporation

Support Your Local Pug

A Pet Palace Mystery

Lane Stone

LYRICAL PRESS
Kensington Publishing Corp.
www.kensingtonbooks.com

Lyrical Press books are published by
Kensington Publishing Corp. 119 West 40th Street New York, NY 10018

First Electronic Edition: August 2018
eISBN-13: 978-1-5161-0192-4
eISBN-10: 1-5161-0192-8

First Print Edition: August 2018
ISBN-13: 978-1-5161-0193-1
ISBN-10: 1-5161-0193-6

Printed in the United States of America

This book is dedicated to all those who have grieved over the loss of a pet, with comforting thoughts and lots of love from our family to yours.

Chapter 1

I had been certain that it was the sound of barking dogs that had yanked me from a deep sleep, but I was wrong. I bolted upright in my bed and grabbed the ringing cell phone. I hit the button, and a man was saying, "We have an alarm going off at the Buckingham Pet Palace. The police department has been notified." He was going for a reassuring tone, but it was way too late for that. I thought about my nighttime employees and the dogs in our care.

In a move somewhere between levitation and acrobatics I was out of bed and pulling on yoga pants and a sweatshirt over the t-shirt I'd slept in. "Call the police—oh, wait, you said you did. I'm on my way."

"What is your password?" he asked.

I hung up without answering, because I had no idea what my password was, and shoved my feet into running shoes and crammed the laces into the sides. My business is at the entrance to the subdivision in Lewes, Delaware, where I live, and in half-formed thoughts I decided I could get there faster running than by getting the Jeep out of the garage and driving over. Abby, my pepper-and-salt Standard Schnauzer, opened her eyes. Her curiosity and intelligence had her tracking my frenetic movements. She would stay awake but saw no need to get excited. Her natural, that is not-cropped, ears were cocked at an angle that told me what she was thinking. Dogs can tell time and she knew three o'clock was too early for a go-out or for breakfast, but since hope springs eternal she was on the lookout for any hint that her bowl might be filled early. I sprinted out the door, shutting down that possibility.

I had my cell phone in my hand and it rang again as I raced down the street. It was one of my night part-time hostesses. Buckingham's employed four of these young mothers, who job shared. They worked two at a time while their husbands were at home, saving babysitter costs, and they were back at home in time to get their kids on the school bus.

"Sue! Have the police called you? Do you know what's happening here?" Taylor Dalton said in a panicked whisper, hardly audible over the high-pitched alarm I heard in the background. "We think he's gone."

"I'm almost there. Are you all right? You're upstairs, aren't you? Did you turn off the elevator?" I hadn't given her time to answer any of the questions, but then I had asked for the most important information last. We had never had a burglary in our three years in business, but we had a plan for the night-timers to follow if someone did break in. Since they spent the night upstairs with the boarding dogs, they were to lock up the elevator, call 9-1-1 and stay put. The door to the back stairway was locked so they didn't have to worry about that point of entry.

"Yeah..."

I didn't hear the rest of what she said now that I was closer to the wailing of the alarm. From the glow of the Victorian-style streetlights, I saw a small car pull out of Buckingham's parking lot on tires best described as insignificant, causing the bottom of the car to scrape the asphalt as it turned onto Village Main Boulevard. Exhaust fumes billowed out the back of it. For the sake of my health, I held my breath. Even with the alarm going off, I could hear its engine clank and complain.

That had to be the burglar.

Personally, I would have gone for more muscle in a getaway car, since the goal was to *get away*. He wasn't traveling at much of a speed, but not for lack of trying. I could hear the old motor straining. I ended the call with Taylor, then held up my phone and aimed it at the clunker. If the gray cloud of the car's vapors dissipated and if the streetlights and the stars filling the sky lit the night well enough, maybe I could photograph the license plate. Then I could blow the image up large enough to get a number. I meant to say, the Lewes police could do that.

The car chugged out of Villages of Five Points. "Oh, what the hell," I said. First, I took a deep breath, knowing the air quality was only going to get worse the closer I got, and then I took off after the car.

In less than a minute, he was at the Savannah Road entrance to the community. That's where I would catch him. Taylor had said "he." Unfortunately, for me at least, the traffic light took pity on the rattletrap and favored it with a green arrow. After the car turned I couldn't photograph the tag, but maybe I could get one of the driver in profile. With aid from the many streetlights on Savannah Road, and the fact that Walgreens is lit up at all hours, I clicked a couple more times.

Then I gave up and started walking back to Buckingham's. With the racket from the motor, I could still hear the car. I turned back around when it slowed in less than a block. Was it stalling out? No, it was turning left onto Old Orchard Road, the street running along the side of the grocery store. I briefly considered cutting through the Weis parking lot but decided that since he would then be driving on a road with neither stoplights nor any traffic to speak of, especially at this hour, I had zero chance of getting close enough to see anything.

My phone rang as I got back to the Buckingham's parking lot. I swiped the screen to answer the call, then dropped the arm holding it to my side. The sight in front of me was such a shock I couldn't speak. The window of one of the outside doors had been smashed and a piece of driftwood propped that door open. A section of a log, five or six inches tall and wide enough to sit on, held the interior doors apart. We had two sets of doors which gave us a sporting chance when a puppy backed out of his collar and decided running from the groomer would be a fun game, or when a grown dog heard the call of the wild.

"Sue! Can you hear me?" It was our police chief, John Turner, and he was on the phone I had dangling by my side.

I listened for what I hadn't heard. A siren. The alarm company had called the police before calling me, so where were my public servants?

"I'm here," I said. "Where are you?"

"Huh? You're here? I don't see you. How did you know to come to Anglers?"

"Why aren't you at Buckingham's?" I asked.

"Why would I be at the Pet Place?" he asked in return.

"It's Pet Palace, as you know, and why would I be at Anglers?" I didn't bother to ask if he meant Anglers Fishing Center or Anglers Marina. I wasn't at either one, so it didn't matter.

"Hold on. The dispatcher wants me." He hung up, leaving me staring at my phone. I guess he didn't know the meaning of hold on. That was fine with me since I didn't have time to talk.

I tucked my phone into the waistband of my yoga pants and went in to my pride and joy—my very successful pet spa. I stepped over the driftwood and sidestepped to get in through the right side exterior door. The interior doors were only separated by the width of the log, which no adult could squeeze through, so I pushed one of the doors open. Once I was through my feet crunched on broken glass. Dry dog food was strewn all over the lobby floor, and I crushed and scattered it underfoot as I made my way to disarm the security system.

I turned to see the door to the storage closet in the hall standing wide open.

I went behind the desk and used the intercom to call my employees on the upper level. "Taylor? Laurie? Can you hear me?"

The phone at the reception desk rang and I answered it. "Is he gone?" It was Taylor.

"Yeah, I saw him drive away. Come on down."

That's when, at last, I heard the police siren. If I wanted to check out my dog food storage closet before the "don't touch anything," yada yada speech, I'd have to move fast.

We had briefly considered installing a lock on the cherry-stained wood door, but felt a deadbolt wasn't in keeping with the royal, or at least British upper-class, ambiance we were trying to create for our pet parents.

I scanned the shelves. We'd need to inventory what was left to learn the exact amount of our loss, but it didn't take a CPA to know that several of the large bags of the gourmet dry food were gone. Two shelves were empty. The cases of canned food didn't seem to have been disturbed.

"Sue! Are you all right?" a baritone voice called from the lobby entrance.

I came out of the storage closet. "I'm fine," I answered.

Chief John Turner stood in the doorway literally scratching his head, as he took in the debris on the floor, before looking up at me. "Good morning," he said with what some of my favorite books would refer to as a sardonic grin. "What have you touched in here?" His winter uniform wasn't really a uniform. He was wearing a white shirt, gray slacks, and a black Lewes Police Department windbreaker.

"Nothing." I walked to him and held out my hands in case he wanted to test for dog food residue.

"I don't hear the alarm. You must have touched the keypad."

"That's all I touched."

"You walked through the dog food," he continued. "We would have liked to check for footprints."

"Well, yeah. But that's all. Really."

"And you moved those doors." He pointed at the interior set of doors.

"Didn't you move them, too?"

"I pushed them open in a way that prevented disturbing any fiber evidence."

"Well, so did I," I said.

He rolled his eyes. "Did you touch anything else?"

"I'm the owner. I've touched everything in here at some time! But, no, I didn't touch anything else this morning." I heard the elevator descending and waited for Taylor and Laurie. The doors parted and I hugged one young woman, and then the other.

I turned to Chief Turner. "They did just what they were taught. They shut down the elevator and stayed upstairs."

"We were so relieved to hear your voice over the intercom," Laurie said.

Chief Turner closed his eyes and took a deep breath. "You touched the intercom," he said. That was my cue to change the subject.

"To get here as fast as you did from Anglers you must have— By the way, what were you doing there at this hour? Are you going fishing?"

"No."

"Why did you think I would be there?" I asked.

"You and I need to head over there as soon as I finish here. I'll explain on the way." Then he turned to Taylor and Laurie. "So, you two sheltered in place?" he asked.

"He told us to," Laurie said.

"He told us to," Taylor said at the same time. "He yelled up at us to stay where we were and no one would get hurt. Then he banged on the elevator door with a gun."

"He had a gun?" Chief Turner's head jerked up at that. "How would you know that? You were upstairs."

Laurie put her hands up, palms out, and gave Taylor an exasperated look. "It was just something metal."

"But it was a man's voice you heard?" Chief Turner asked.

"A man who is into very old movies," I added.

Simultaneously they saw the state of the lobby floor and the doors.

"Oh, no!" Laurie cried.

"You two are okay, and that's all that matters," I assured them. "I don't care about the burglary."

Chief Turner had his notepad out and was writing without looking at it, a life skill that could come in handy from time to time. Or maybe making heads or tails of it later was the amazing part. "You weren't burgled. Since they were threatened," he said, stopping to point at Taylor and Laurie, "you were robbed."

"Thanks for clearing that up," I said.

"I'll get a crime scene team out here," Turner said, completely ignoring my first-rate sarcastic remark.

I turned back to Taylor and Laurie. "I tried to chase him. Did you see his car from the window?"

"There was too much pollution coming out of it to see much," Taylor said, making a face. "We heard it and went to the window to look out."

"You could hear his car from up there?" I asked.

They both said they had, laughing nervously but starting to relax.

"People in Rehoboth probably heard it," Laurie said. "He left it running. I guess that's why we didn't hear the breaking glass or when he made this mess."

John was making notes as they spoke. "Did you see the make or model?"

"Tiny and foreign," Laurie answered.

"Stinky and small," Taylor said.

The chief's pencil stopped. "You two are practically expert witnesses, you know that?"

"It looked like it was from another century," I said. I glanced at Taylor and Laurie to see if he had hurt their feelings, but they were laughing.

Was Turner trying to be funny? Or condescending and superior? He had done it again. Would I ever go out with him? Hell to the no.

Chapter 2

"Sue?" It was Shelby Ryan, my assistant manager. "Are you in there?"

"Stay outside!" Chief Turner called.

"Stay! Stay! Stay!" Shelby said.

"Yeah, that's what I said." The police chief was taking notes, his back to the door.

"Oh, no!" I knew what was coming and turned to Taylor and Laurie. "She has the puppies with her." On Christmas Day, Shelby's Bernese Mountain Dog—poetically named Bernice—had a litter of eight puppies. Shelby, and her husband, Jeffrey, had three left. And those three had smelled the food that was covering the lobby floor. They tumbled over the board holding the inner doors apart and ran in. When their claws got to the pilfered food, they began skidding, trying to catch kibble in their mouths as they slid.

"My evidence!" Turner yelled. Then he saw Bernice. His mouth dropped open at the sight of the one-hundred-pound dog.

Bernice was on a leash and when Shelby commanded her to stay, she did, though she did look longingly at the buffet she was missing out on as she stood with her head and neck between the doors. She, like most of her breed, had what was known as a dry mouth, which meant she didn't drool. Bernice's *tight* lips meant the lobby entrance would stay dry, more or less.

Taylor and Laurie each picked up a puppy. I picked up the third.

"Sorry," Shelby said. We have a strict no leash–no lobby rule. "I raced out the door when the alarm company called. Sue, they said you didn't give them the password." For her to have driven with Bernice and her puppies loose in the car instead of crated or harnessed told me she had been as worried as I had been at the thought of Taylor and Laurie here during a break-in.

The flashing lights of a second Lewes police department car lit up our small parking lot.

Chief Turner looked at Bernice, then at Shelby. "Would you mind, uh, doing something with that?" He obviously wanted to meet with the new police officer on the scene, but the dog's head, the size of a football, still filled the space between the two interior doors.

"Sure. Sorry, I forgot," Shelby said and returned her dog to the van. This was the van we had used to chauffeur dogs until one of our employees was found murdered in it last year. We figured the good people of Lewes wouldn't want to see it around town and besides, it seemed disrespectful of the dead. We had the title to the Honda van transferred to Shelby, and she transferred the title of her Prius to Buckingham's. The van was our signature golf-course-green, and she had it painted white. We had the Buckingham Pet Palace logo painted on her Prius and we were good to go. Sometimes we had to make more than one trip for morning pickups or afternoon drop-offs, but that was okay. A small-business owner that wasn't flexible was soon out of business.

Chief Turner carefully worked his way through the doors to get outside, where, except for the patrol car headlights, it was still dark.

As soon as Shelby came back inside she stretched her arms wide for a group hug.

"Shelby, your hair is as big as a person," Taylor said, holding up a strand of thick, curly, red locks, and towering over her. Shelby was just over five feet tall. "Did you know that?"

"If you're giving me a hard time, I guess everybody's okay," she said.

"It might take Chief Turner a while to get over seeing Bernice," I said.

"So Lewes Five-O hasn't gotten over his fear of dogs?" she whispered. That's only one of the nicknames we have for our town's oh-so-serious, and dangerously handsome police chief.

"Doesn't look like it," I said.

"Guess what?" Laurie asked. "Sue tried to chase the burglar's car."

"I would have paid good money to see that," Shelby said.

"It was so old for a minute I thought I had a shot."

Chief Turner was back inside. "Can anyone tell me anything else about the vehicle?"

"The paint job was so faded that even if there had been more light, I doubt I could say what color it was," I said. "I saw some rust, if that helps. It looked like a little clown car."

"A little clown car," he mimicked. He added that to his trusty notepad, then closed it again.

I had been about to show him the photos I had taken of the car, but figured I should look at them in private before sharing them with Mr. Smart Ass, in case there wasn't anything to see. Sure, I would have loved to be the person who could say, "That car? It's a '96 Corvette." Or, "Hey, look, everybody, there goes a '67 El Camino made in Atlanta." But I'm not. Never would be. I can, however, identify dog breeds all day long.

"Can you come with me to Anglers now?"

"Why?" I asked, surely a reasonable question.

"I, uh, have a situation," he let the sentence trail off.

"Officer Statler will wait here for the crime scene team." He pointed over his shoulder to the uniformed officer, a young woman, standing behind him.

Rather than hang around for my answer, he gave further instructions to her. "Take statements from the two late–shift employees." He gave the dog food on the floor a look that showed how profoundly the puppies had hurt him, then went out to the parking lot.

I didn't have my watch on, but I guessed it was about four o'clock. "Shelby, if I'm not back in an hour, would you walk and feed Abby?"

"Of course," she answered. "Anglers? Is he taking you fishing?"

"I don't think so," I said. "I have no idea why he wants to go there."

"He's tried every other way to get you to go out with him. Maybe he thought that would work."

"Does he fish?" Laurie asked, with a doubtful look on her face.

I shrugged. "Maybe. Who knows? The guy is so private it's like he's in a witness protection program. Taylor and Laurie, do any of the boarders need extra TLC? What were the dogs doing while all this was going on?"

"All of them woke up and a few were curious. No one got upset or even barked," Laurie said.

"Hmm," I said. "They must not have thought you two were in any danger, or felt threatened. I'm surprised the high-pitched sound of the alarm didn't upset some of them. Good job, ladies!"

I handed Shelby the puppy I was still snuggling and went to meet Chief Turner outside. He was waiting for me by his police cruiser. Our town, with a population of around three thousand, had a handful of these white cars with the yellow and black bands painted on the two front doors. The city's coat of arms, which had been shamelessly copied from Lewes, in Sussex, England, was painted on both sides of the cars, too. He walked around the rear of the car and opened the door for me. "That's what you wear in February?"

The sweatshirt had been adequate when I was scared to death. Now, not so much. "I'll go home and get a jacket and meet you at Anglers."

"Here," he said, shrugging out of his windbreaker. "Take this."

I graciously took the jacket, and got in the car, looking back at Buckingham's, where I should be and wanted to be. I didn't put it on—I was still leaving my options open, though we were driving out of the parking lot. "I really should stay here and clean up to get ready to open."

"You can't clean up until the crime scene team gets done."

"And they'll be through before seven o'clock?" That's when we open on weekdays.

"I think so." We waited for the light to change, both lost in our thoughts. I was wondering who around here would steal dog food. Then we turned onto Savannah Road and headed for downtown Lewes. On that stretch of road the speed limit lowered several times. I noticed that he obeyed each and every sign. If the police chief couldn't speed, who could? Still, he drove at thirty-five miles per hour then twenty-five. Cute.

His avoiding telling me why we were going to Anglers? Not cute. It was too early for the store to be open. That meant we were going to the dock.

"So, what do you hear from Lady Anthea?" he asked.

Lady Anthea Fitzwalter and I are co-owners of the Buckingham Pet Palace. Her brother was a duke, her grandmother was lady-in-waiting to the queen, and her house, actually an estate, had a name. It's Frithsden. At first, she was a silent partner. Using her name and photographs of her home, gardens, and dogs gave Buckingham's royal cred. I paid her a percentage of the profits. Last August she visited and we bonded over solving the murder of Henry Canon.

"She'll be here tomorrow," I answered. "Last year the American Kennel Club approved a Trick Dog titling program. She'll be teaching a one-week trick class and an agility class."

"What is that?"

"It's a timed, obstacle course a dog—"

"Oh, it's for dogs?" he interrupted.

I rolled my eyes, more for my own benefit since it was still dark outside. "No, it's for men we're considering dating."

"Will she mind not being the only VIP in Lewes?"

"Who else is in town?" I asked.

"Howard Fourie, the CEO of the management company running Friday's celebration."

"You're not really comparing her centuries-old family name and title to Mr. Edutainer, are you?" I loaded all the derision I felt for the educational and entertainment project into my question. When there were no pet parents in Buckingham's we strung out M-i-s-t-e-r E-d-u-t-a-i-n-e-r like circus barkers.

"Mr. Fourie wants to help Lewes celebrate some local history. But what I want to know is what kind of town celebrates the twenty-year anniversary of finding the bottom of a broken wine bottle?"

"Surely you know more about the discovery of the artifacts from the British supply ship than that." I didn't wait for his reply. "Are you stalling for time? Why don't you want to tell me why we're going to Anglers at this extreme hour?"

"We're going there because that's where the launch will pick us up to take us to the Harbor of Refuge Lighthouse. I need your help with something."

"Look, you're going to have to tell me more. I'd rather be at Buckingham's. That's where I need to be." If we had been at a stop sign I swear I would have jumped out and run back.

"I'm sorry. I'm trying to process a few things at once." He ran his hand over his short hair. "This morning I was about to call you and explain why we needed to go to the lighthouse when the alarm call came in. I was worried about you."

"You need to go," I said.

"Huh?"

"The light's green." There was a car behind us but since it was a police car sitting still at the light, the prudent motorist had resisted honking his horn.

Chief Turner waved an apology and drove on. We crossed the drawbridge over the canal and turned left. We drove to the end of Anglers Road, right up to the big blue Anglers Fishing Center sign.

"Why do you need *my* help with something going on at the lighthouse? I could give you the phone number for the president of the lighthouse foundation. Or you could call the Army Corps of Engineers since they own the Breakwater," I said.

"I'm pretty sure you're the best person for this particular situation. A pilot was on his way to a freighter and swears he heard a dog barking out on the Harbor of Refuge Lighthouse."

Chapter 3

"No one on the pilot boat saw a *person* on the lighthouse? The Coast Guard maintains the foghorn and light, since it's still an active aid to navigation. I guess someone could have taken their dog along," I suggested.

"No," Chief Turner said from behind me, as we boarded the fifty-two-foot boat. It was still dark. "I checked with the commandant. None of his folks are out there."

Sun King could have held thirty-five passengers, maybe more, but it was just the two of us plus the captain, who stood near the ladder, and his crew of three.

"Thanks for doing this, Captain Westlake," Chief Turner said, as they shook hands.

"Happy to help. Call me Captain Sandy. Welcome aboard, Sue."

He handed us each an orange life vest. I held mine instead of pulling the strap over my neck. When you have your own personal flotation device, these foam versions are the equivalent of the rented bowling shoe.

From the lights on board and on the deck, I could see the tall man had sandy hair and a friendly face. The name was familiar, and it sounded like he knew me. "You have a Shih Tzu, right?" I asked.

He looked down and lowered his voice. "That's my wife's, soon-to-be ex-wife's, dog."

John looked at me with an *I rest my case* look. I looked back at him with a *we'll discuss this later* look. It was hardly fair to say the Shih Tzu had caused the divorce.

"I'll get you something to keep you warm," Captain Sandy said and turned to go below deck. He returned with a polyurethane anorak and handed it to me. When he handed me the waterproof jacket, I noticed the size of his arms. His biceps had the circumference of a Shih Tzu.

I gave Chief Turner his jacket back. He was going to need it. We took our seats on a bench in front of the wheelhouse, trying to get out of the wind and safe from the spray for the trip.

I hadn't said much since we boarded and got seated. "How close do pilot boats get to the lighthouse?" Then I answered my own question, "I guess it depends on where he was coming from. What kind of dog...?"

I shivered and Chief Turner put his arm around my shoulders to keep me warm. That was new. "I wasn't hinting for you to do that, you know," I said.

"I know," John said, with a chuckle.

"Now that we have that settled, you're sure no crew member of the pilot boat actually *saw* a dog? Sometimes sound does funny things on the ocean," I said.

"Do you and your friends ever hear *funny things* when you're on your surfboards?"

The smart-mouth, patronizing way he said "funny things" reminded me once again why I had never gone out with him in the six months since we met. I was this close to making up some ghost dog legend, but instead I said, "All the time, but then *we're* drinking. Yep, sometimes we're SUI, surfing under the influence."

He smirked and then something, turned out it was someone, over my shoulder caught his eye. I turned to see Captain Sandy standing at the railing. He turned and went back to the wheel. John reverted back to his default mode, which is sober to the point of having an alpha-dog sense of duty. "Let's talk about your robbery. How much money are we talking here? What's the value of the merchandise you lost?"

"Five or six hundred dollars."

"Is it dog food or pure China White?" he asked.

"Huh?"

"Heroin, but never mind. I had no idea people spent that much to feed those—" He turned and saw the look on my face and stopped. He took a deep breath. "Sorry, I forgot our deal." He still had his arm around me so our faces were close.

I nodded, then looked out at the ocean. The Harbor of Refuge Lighthouse was out there. Everything was out there. "You said you would give dogs a chance. Remember?"

"In exchange for you giving me a chance. You haven't exactly lived up to your part of the bargain either," he said.

I had nothing to say to that.

"Tomorrow night?" he asked.

"Tomorrow night, what?"

"Let's have dinner tomorrow night."

"Okay," I said.

He did a double take, then gave me a skeptical look. "Really?"

I held out my hand to shake his and clinch the deal.

He took my hand in his. "Finally! Yes!" he said in his deep baritone voice, laughing. He had a good laugh, I had to admit. "This has been some morning."

"It's been a *busy* morning. We had a dog food theft at my place, plus whatever is going on out here." I shivered again. Something wasn't right and I tried to decide if I would tell Chief Turner that I was worried. If I told him my misgivings would he still go to the lighthouse for the dog?

Then he was leaning in closer. I was aware of the sky lightening up. We were traveling west, so we wouldn't see the sun come up even if we were on the water that long, but there was a rosiness surrounding us. "See how pink the sky looks?" I asked.

He nodded.

"It's called nautical twilight. We're between night and day, and the sun hasn't risen but it's still lighting the sky. Just a little."

He smiled and nodded again, and leaned closer. "Maybe," he said, "like us?"

I leaned in, thinking how my lips would feel in a few seconds. Suddenly I jerked back. "We're being set up," I said.

"Practically the whole town has been trying to get us together," he said, with a hurt look on his face.

"That's not what I'm talking about. Think about all that's happened this morning. Someone wants us out of the way."

"I can understand someone wanting me out of town, but why you?" he asked.

"Excuse me?"

"You own the Pet Place," he said.

I sat up straight, feeling the cold again. "It's Pet Palace," I reminded him.

He stood and looked out at the ocean.

"Maybe you're right and it was just a crazy morning. Breaking into Buckingham's and threatening my employees would ordinarily be a sure way to keep me *there*." I was talking to his back.

He twisted around and said, "If someone arranged this to get me—or us—out of town, he picked a surefire way to do it." Then he turned back and looked straight ahead. "What is going on out there?" he asked. I think more to himself than to me.

"You said someone had abandoned a dog on the lighthouse."

"But why would anyone do that? Why not leave him on a road, or a parking lot? Isn't that what people usually do?"

I flinched. I wanted to say something about animal rescue organizations but the thought of abandoned dogs made me wince, and I felt physical pain, like a punch to my gut.

Chief Turner was still talking. "I shouldn't have asked you to come. There might be someone hiding inside the lighthouse."

"I'm glad you called me. We can't leave a dog out there, so you'll need me to get him aboard." I didn't have to bring up the fact that our big, tough police chief was afraid of dogs. "I just realized I didn't bring a leash." I looked around. "Hmm, I wonder if there's something on board I can use. I could make a harness out of three lengths of line but with any luck the dog is wearing a collar."

"And I need binoculars. I'll go talk to the captain," Chief Turner said and began making his way to the wheelhouse.

"Remember to call it line instead of rope."

"I'll keep that in mind." He stopped in his tracks and turned around to face me. "You know I've been on the water before?"

"Uh, no." I knew very little about our police chief's life before he moved to Lewes.

Suddenly the wind kicked up and the temperature lowered. We were still in the Delaware Bay but we were nearing the Atlantic Ocean. I lifted my face.

"You're happy out here, aren't you?" John was back with a pair of binoculars, and a line loosely looped over his arm, which he dropped to the deck next to my feet.

"Yes, I get why a dog likes to have his head out of a car window. Try it," I said, knowing there was no way he was going to.

He walked to the bow and scanned the horizon with the binoculars, a slow arc to the starboard side then sweeping back to port.

"Can you see anything?" I asked.

"Not a thing," he answered as he returned to sit beside me, and offered me the binoculars.

I didn't bother to go to the bow. Instead I leaned forward on the bench. "All I can see is fog." Then there was a break in the mist and the lighthouse magically appeared. The top two-thirds of the Harbor of Refuge Lighthouse was white, the caisson base was black and she sat on a bed of concrete at the south end of the Delaware breakwater. Then I was back to worrying about the dog alone on the lighthouse. "What time did the pilot call you?"

"The call came into the station around 3:30."

"I hope he's still there. Sometimes a dog will jump in the water if he's thirsty enough. Once Abby almost jumped off a bridge." I lowered my head and pinched the bridge of my nose. "The Harbor of Refuge Lighthouse got a new dock last year. Hopefully water splashed up from between the planks or the grate and he got a taste of the salt water, just enough to make him stay where he is."

The foghorn blast surprised both of us. Since it was coming from seventy-six feet above us, the volume wasn't what had startled us, it was the feeling that the sound had come from nowhere. "It does that to me every time!" I laughed. "Get ready, there'll be two bursts every thirty seconds."

I darted to the bow and looked through the binoculars again. "Look!" I pointed at the small brown dog pacing on the concrete deck of the lighthouse. "There he is!" I turned back to Chief Turner, but he wasn't there. "John?"

Voices traveled up to me from the port side of the boat. Chief Turner was talking to the captain who was nodding at whatever he was being told. Then he walked back to me and Captain Sandy Westlake went to speak to a crew member, who had been waiting aft.

"He's going to go around before we dock," Chief Turner said, taking the binoculars from me. He raised them to his face and looked out at the light.

"You really think this might be a trap?" I asked.

He shrugged. "I heard you call me John," was his non-answer.

I rolled my eyes. "See the dog? It's a Pug."

"Yeah."

Captain Sandy pulled back on the throttle and we drifted closer. The tall structure dwarfed us. From a distance, a lighthouse charms, but up close it thrills. The captain revved the engine and the *Sun King* turned for us to motor the half circle to the other side, up to the breakwater. The binoculars John held moved from the base, to each of the windows, then back again. Finally, he looked at Captain Sandy in the wheelhouse and nodded. We went back to the other side of the lighthouse and the new twenty-foot by twenty-foot dock.

As the crew performed their docking routine, I observed the dog. And he watched me, more curious than wary. His ears and tail, though it was curled, were relaxed. "Hi there," I said, now that I knew we could be friends. I could see he wore a red collar, but no tags.

John climbed onto the lighthouse dock and I followed. I stopped when I saw the worried expression on his face.

"Let's hurry," he said. "No one in law enforcement believes in coincidences."

"You're thinking if you weren't lured *here,* there must be something going on in Lewes?" I asked.

Chapter 4

The Pug came when I had reached my hand out to him. I had picked him up and after a long, sweet sigh, he slumped against me. Transferring him from the lighthouse dock to the boat was going fine—until he saw Captain Sandy. The tired dog was no longer docile. He snarled at him, adding a low growl just to be sure he was understood. His ears were pinned back to his head and his body was a ball of spring-loaded tension.

"Settle!" I said, not raising my voice but making it sound like the command it was.

Time froze. Until that point I had been only vaguely aware of Chief Turner watching all this. The volume of the growl was lower, but the dog was trembling in my arms. Both told me this dog wasn't acting aggressively, instead he was fearful. He was afraid but not scared straight. He would defend himself if he had to. I held up a hand to let Chief Turner know everything was under control. "It's okay," I whispered to both, the dog and the man.

I needed the dog to trust me enough to take his mind off whatever he was afraid of. Children can stress dogs, but second on the list are big men. A crewmember had thoughtfully brought a bowl of water to us. The dog was exhausted and maybe dehydrated so I moved the water bowl closer to him with my foot as a distraction and a bribe. He took his eyes off the captain and looked down at it for a brief second. The growling stopped. He squirmed which I took as a request for me to put him on the deck, which I did. He stood by my foot, but didn't allow himself any water.

"Good boy," I said. He looked at me again then went back to eyeing the boat captain, all the while keeping his guard up. "Can we get underway now?" I asked, mostly to get the man out of the dog's line of vision.

"Sure thing," Captain Sandy said and returned to the wheelhouse.

The Pug drank the bowl dry, as I stood near the rail and watched. "Who are you?"

At the sound of my voice, he looked at me with that wistful and vulnerable look Pugs' faces have. I went to the bench and sat. "Come." The dog joined me and I petted him as a reward for obeying the command.

Neither Chief Turner, now standing at the bow, nor I, spoke. I was thinking about the lack of rabies and registration tags on the dog's collar. I kept Abby's identifying jewelry on a key ring. Personally I wouldn't want constant jangling near my ears and I projected this need for calm onto her. Did the Pug's owner agree, or was the dog unvaccinated and unregistered? From there I went to wondering if the dog had a microchip we could scan to get him reunited with his family.

The chief was thinking whatever police chiefs think about. Then he turned to face me and said, "You'll need to come to the station to give a statement on your break-in."

I thought back to the mess I'd left my staff to clean up. "Oh, no. I have to get back to Buckingham's." I took my cell phone out of my pants pocket and held it up. "I'll text-ify."

"No such thing."

"I'm pretty sure it *is* a thing."

He shook his head, but couldn't stop himself from grinning.

I held my phone higher like it was evidence. Then it rang. I casually answered it, trying to cover up how it had startled me.

"Sue?" It was Shelby and she was whispering.

"I can hardly hear you."

"I came to your house to take Abby out for her walk and bring her to Buckingham's. I'm parked in your next-door neighbor's driveway. You know, the people who are never here."

"Why aren't you parked in my driveway?" I asked.

"That car—you know, the worst getaway car, ever—it's in your driveway."

The stunned look on my face brought Chief Turner to my side. Mystery dog or no mystery dog by my foot. "That car from this morning's robbery is at my house," I whispered. Actually, it was more like a stage whisper because anything less on the open water is audible only to dogs.

"Is there anyone in it?" he asked, as he pulled his own phone out of his jacket pocket.

"Shelby, I'll put you on speaker."

"I don't see anyone. Sue, I'm worried about Abby. If he's broken into your house, she's being held hostage."

John looked straight up at the sky and then shook his head before speaking again. "Tell Shelby to get away from there," he said through clenched teeth. "I'll send officers." Then he told them to go to my address, which he knew. By heart. I'd have to ask him about that later.

"Shelby, did you hear what he said about leaving?" I asked.

"You're breaking up." Knowing what it means when I tell someone that, I took her off speaker.

"You there?" I asked.

"Yeah. Sue, don't worry about Abby. Bernice and I are going around back."

"Be careful!" I wanted her to wait for the police, though I probably would have done just as she had. And let's face it, if you were going into a possibly dangerous situation you could do worse than have a hundred-pound dog for a bodyguard.

That got a look from John and I twisted away from him. I heard Shelby say, "Let's go, girl." Next I heard her car door open and close. I heard Bernice's heavy panting. They were on the move.

In another minute Shelby said, "There's no one on the screened-in porch. I'm going to look in the window."

"Ieeee," Shelby screamed. Bernice barked twice, loud but she almost sounded playful.

"What happened?" I yelled.

"I'm okay. Abby jumped up at the window and scared me. I'm looking in." I waited and imagined her scanning my family room. "I don't see anyone and Abby looks fine. Wait, what's that noise?" Then she said, "That car just started."

"Shelby, what's going on?" No answer. "Shelby?" I became aware of something near, almost touching, my shoulder.

"She didn't get the hell out of there like I said, did she?" Chief Turner demanded.

I shook my head, and brought him up-to-date. I put the call back on speaker as a peace offering, though I wasn't sure it was seen as such, what with certain people not knowing how to express gratitude. Then I heard the sound of a siren over the phone.

"Sue?" It was Shelby.

"I'm here," I said, relief flooding through me that she was okay.

"The car's gone."

"That's great!"

"Not really," Shelby said. "There's a body in front of your garage door." John and I looked at one another.

"We're on our way," John said.

I verified that she had heard him. My phone beeped that I had a new text, and I swiped the screen to read it. I read it aloud because I wanted both Chief Turner and Shelby to hear the latest. "This is from Rick Ziegler. He says he can't supply our raw dog food until this afternoon. Someone broke in at Raw-k & Roll and...well, they either burgled or robbed him. Either way, his stuff's gone."

"Not my jurisdiction," Chief Turner said.

"His dog food costs even more than mine since it's raw food, handmade with locally sourced, organic ingredients," I said.

"Still not my jurisdiction."

"Okay, but it adds to those coincidences you said law enforcement officers don't like." My phone made a different sound and I looked at the screen. Lady Anthea Fitzwalter was calling. I said goodbye to Shelby, then answered the new call.

Lady Anthea was talking before I even said hello. "Sue, I need to tell you something. I apologize and have to say that I don't know how this came about."

She hesitated and I jumped in before she could say any more—before she could add another complication to my perfectly ordered life. "Shelby just found a dead body."

"I'm on my way! Don't start without me!"

Chapter 5

"I know him," I said. I was kneeling by my garage door, studying the elderly man lying dead on my driveway.

Chief Turner had made a zone of calm and privacy for me to view the lifeless form. Turner's body language got more done than the average person's. Magazine articles said crossed arms meant he or she liked or didn't like you, or whatever it was the studies by experts had decided. John Turner's body language could calm people down, make them talk, or that morning in front of my house, clear a space.

The man was crumpled on his side with a bloody gash on his head, left ear, and neck. The arm under his body reached above his head.

"What's his name?" he asked.

"Beats me," I said.

"You said you knew him."

"Everybody knows him. He works at Mozart's, the German deli on Second Street."

"Let me see," Shelby said, scooting in. "You're right!"

I looked up into the sunlight at Chief Turner, who was checking his watch. I wanted to ask him if he had a bus to catch. A pill to take? Was the dead man keeping him from something more important? Was he that unfeeling?

"He sings opera while he waits on customers," I explained. "How could you live here all these months and not know him?" There was more. I knew something else about him, but that information was determined to stay out of reach. Did I know his family? Had he brought his dog to Buckingham's? Maybe he'd been at the Pet Parent Appreciation Gala? I closed my eyes and tried to imagine him somewhere other than the deli. Nope, I only knew him from where he worked. I opened my eyes and looked for a clue. He wore a faded plaid shirt, with long sleeves that ended at an unbuttoned cuff and a skinny wrist. "No wallet?" I asked.

Chief Turner gave an exasperated shake of his head. He jerked his thumb to the other officers on the scene. "They told me he had nothing at all in his pockets."

"What's this?" I said. Then I figured it out. "There's blood on his fingers."

John knelt down next to me for a closer look but didn't say anything. I got up and moved away, to give them room to work. I walked to the middle of my driveway, making my way through waiting police officers and other official-looking types. Shelby followed me. Bernice was close by her side, now on a leash and with zero slack. The dog was enthralled with the yellow crime scene tape that fluttered in the breeze. It had been strung on orange cones lined up on the street the length of my front yard, and then up the side property lines.

"Dana came in and she's babysitting the mystery dog until one of us gets back," Shelby said.

We planned to take the Pug to our local vet, Lewes 24-hour Pet Care, to be scanned for a chip. In the meantime, he was quarantined, since we didn't know his vaccination status.

"She doesn't have classes today?" I asked. Dana, a senior at Cape Henlopen High, was one of Buckingham's afternoon part-timers.

"She saw the police cars on her way to school and came in. When Mason told her we had another dead body, there was no way she was leaving. I told her we would be back soon, so she wouldn't miss too much school." Shelby hesitated. "You know she still says she wants to be a detective after we asked her to help us with that internet research last year."

I leaned over and gave Bernice a scratch under her chin. Her tricolor coat was thick and slightly wavy. She was sitting like such a good girl. I was waiting for John to say something about the dog contaminating the crime scene, but he hadn't. Instead he looked around and with a slight nod gave permission for the body to be covered, in preparation for being moved, then walked up to us. "Shelby, let's go over this again. When you arrived the car we believe was involved in this morning's robbery at the Pet Place was parked in the driveway, correct?"

"Pet Palace," I interjected.

"Yes, that's right," Shelby said.

"You didn't see anyone inside the vehicle?"

"No, I didn't."

He looked at the street, then to the garage door, then back to Shelby. "If the body had been lying there when the car was parked here, would you have been able to see it?"

She motioned to my neighbor's house. "We went around the other side of that house to get to the backyard, so I wouldn't have seen what was in front of the car." She hesitated, then said, "I don't know, I mean, it's a tiny car, so maybe I could have if I had looked down."

The clanking of metal made all three of us look back at the deceased man. The stretcher was raised to waist height of the three people who would take him away. "Where are they taking him?" I asked. All of a sudden it was important to me. More important than the break-in, or the dog on the lighthouse, or the robbery at Raw-k & Roll. I knew that something would be missing when he was gone. For a second there I thought I was going to remember what else I knew about the guy but no such luck. "Has his family been told what happened?"

Chief Turner looked at his watch again. "No, for now he's a John Doe. Since you told me where he works I'll wait for the deli to open and go over there."

"Oh," I said, glad I hadn't given him grief about checking the time.

He rubbed the back of his hand back and forth across his forehead. "We know there were two people here."

"You're just now ruling out suicide?" I asked.

"I'll ignore that," Chief Turner said. "I was about to say that the car you described was too small for two people to be hiding in it without their heads being seen. Somebody drove the car away. But then how did the second person get here?"

"Where were they when Shelby and Bernice were here?" I asked myself.

Chief Turner motioned for a man and woman waiting in the street by the crime scene van to join us. "Fred, dust for fingerprints on all the doors. Marie, look around all sides of the house for tamped-down grass." He pointed at the far side of my house. "Start over there."

The gurney was pushed down the driveway on the way to the ambulance.

"You think he and who ever drove the car away came together?" I asked. "And then, what? Got in an argument? One killed the other?" I pulled my phone out of my pants pocket and began scrolling through the photos.

"That's a possible scenario. Wait, we're not starting the text-ifying thing again, are we?"

I rolled my eyes. "I'm checking the photographs I took this morning."

"You took photographs of the car used in a murder and a burglary—"

"Robbery," I corrected him.

"And you're just now showing them to me?"

I held my phone up for him to see. "Look, just one driver." I heard a noise coming from my living room window. It was Abby scratching to let me know she hadn't been taken out for her walk. I went up the driveway to the garage door.

"Yes, someone drove the car away," Chief Turner said. "Would you send me those photographs? Where are you going?"

"Inside. This is crazy. Why would he come to my house? And you don't even know if he was killed here, do you?"

Chief Turner reluctantly agreed with that.

"I want to see if anyone went inside—which I seriously doubt! And I need to check on Abby." As I ranted, I raised the cover of the garage door opener keypad then froze. It was covered in blood.

Chapter 6

"The blood on his fingers..." I didn't finish the sentence because I was imagining what had happened here—here at my house. "There's no blood on the cover." I saw him come to the keypad. The top row of buttons was now dyed brownish red. "He opened the cover, then he was hit on the head." Sure, there were other possibilities, but this felt right.

John, standing behind me, reached over and put both of his big paws on my hands and lowered my arms before I disturbed anything. The touch had been so gentle I could have imagined it, except for the way my skin felt.

He picked up the story. "He put his hand up to his head where he was struck, then tried the keypad, but collapsed before he could gain entry."

We had been looking each other in the eye. "We're thinking alike," I said. "This is just like the last case we solved."

Chief Turner took the notepad out of his jacket pocket. "You didn't have a case *then*, and you don't have one *now*." He spoke slowly, and in a singsong rhythm.

Shelby snorted a laugh that said: *we'll see about that*. More than a few of the officers snickered too, then tried to turn theirs into coughs when Chief Turner swung his head around to them.

"I have someone who thought he could get into my house. He had, or at least thought he had, my passcode. Why else would he try?"

"Can you go inside through the front door?" John asked.

After seeing the blood, I had forgotten I was about to go in to take care of Abby. "Sure."

The uniformed officer, Officer Statler, from this morning at Buckingham's, cleared her throat. She was waiting a few feet away.

"I think she needs to talk to us," I said, giving her a smile.

"I'm pretty sure it's me she was waiting for," Chief Turner said.

"Whatever," I said.

"Whaddya got?" Chief Turner asked.

"Looks like someone ran across the front yard," she said.

I interrupted her. "With or without a dog?" I motioned for Shelby to join us.

"Without. In this direction." She pointed to the right. "He or she ran along that side of the house and then doubled back to the front yard."

"As a guess, does the shoe size look like it could have been him?" I pointed back to where the ambulance had been parked.

"We're taking photographs now," she said. I was wondering how long Chief Turner was going to let me go on.

"Suuuuue?" I had my answer. He was standing next to me, starting a low boil.

"That's all for now, Officer Statler," I said.

"Sue!" He had blown. "That's all period!"

"I'll get Abby, then I'll be at Buckingham's," I said. "If you need me." I added that because I couldn't help myself.

"Sue, I'll take Bernice home and come back," Shelby said.

Chief Turner pointed his pen at the dog. "She knows not to leave town, right?"

Whenever he joked like that I felt myself thaw—a little. Too bad they were outnumbered about a hundred to one by his harsh remarks. I walked to the front porch and let myself in. Abby had had a very confusing morning and she let me know it. She was sitting just inside the front door, staring at me and waiting for an explanation.

"You don't lock your front door?" Chief Turner was right on my heels.

"This is Lewes," I reminded him as I leaned over to pet Abby. I walked to the back porch with Abby following, leaving Chief Turner to check out each room—there weren't many—for signs of something. I opened the door to the screened-in porch and Abby ran outside for her "go-out," as we like to call it.

"Let's get some breakfast," I said when we were back inside.

"Thanks, but I've eaten." I guess he was satisfied the premises were secure since he was standing in the family room waiting for us.

"I was talking to Abby," I said. She had taken off and was waiting for me by her bowls.

"Sue, with that," he said, motioning in the general direction of the garage, "I'm going to have to put in a lot of hours the next few days. Can we take a rain check on dinner tomorrow night?"

"Of course!" I said. "Wait a minute, are you canceling our dinner because the body was found here? I can't be a suspect because I was with you!"

"Technically, that would depend on the time of death, but, of course, I don't suspect you."

I went back to filling Abby's bowls.

"Well, do you want to go get some breakfast?" he asked.

"Thanks, but I need to get to Buckingham's. I have to place a dog food order, take the mystery dog to the vet to see if he has a chip...."

"Look, I hope you don't feel uncomfortable because of what happened on the boat," he said.

"What happened on the boat?"

"When you tried to kiss me," he said.

"Whaaaaat?" I yelled. "In your dreams! I didn't try to kiss you!" I realized I was holding Abby's bowl and she was looking at it longingly so I lowered it to the floor. "You tried to kiss me!"

I was yelling at myself. He'd gone.

Chapter 7

"Oh, no!" Dana cried when she heard my tale of the blood on the keypad of my garage door opener. We were huddled behind the reception desk at Buckingham's.

"His fingerprints were on the top row of keys and he died or passed out or something before he could enter the last digit," I explained.

Shelby jumped in to say, "Sue, first, make a list of everyone you've given that code to. Then you've got to change it. That guy was *this* close to breaking into your house." She held her thumb and forefinger an inch apart. "Sure, he was probably trying to get away from his killer but still—"

"Wait, wait…" Dana tried again to get a word in.

"Why do I need to change it now? The person that had the passcode is dead."

"He must have gotten it from somebody since obviously you didn't give it to him," Shelby answered.

"Listen to meeeeee!" Dana wailed.

Shelby and I turned to her. She was young and we had no business barreling ahead like we had been doing. "I apologize," I said.

Dana took a deep breath. "Your passcode is 1-2-3-4, isn't it?"

"Yeah," I said and looked around. "How did you know? Is it written down somewhere?"

"No, but half the people on the planet use that as a passcode. He was guessing," she said. "That's why only the top row of buttons had blood on them."

"Ooooooh," Shelby and I said at the same time and with equal sheepishness.

We turned when we heard the front door open. Mason came in carrying the Pug. They had been to Lewes 24-Hour Pet Care to see if the little guy had a chip.

"Brrr," he said. "I think it's colder in here than outside."

"I have a call in to Class Glass," Shelby said.

Shelby and I were wearing green Buckingham Pet Palace pullovers. Dana still had on her leather jacket. It was a bright and sunny day, but the cold air coming in through the wrecked doors meant we were chilly.

My cell phone rang and I waved a greeting at Mason and answered the call.

"What did you find out?" Shelby asked.

I turned to listen to my caller, not waiting to hear what Mason said since I assumed the answer was that there was no chip. The morning we were having wasn't going to have a piece of good news pop up.

"I have the name of the deceased," Chief Turner said. "I have someone tracking down his next of kin."

"That's progress. What's his name?" I asked.

"Sue, you know I'm not allowed to say."

"I told you, I already know him. I just don't know his name."

"If I tell you, will you let me know if you think of anything else about him or his associates?"

"Of course," I promised.

"I don't want this all over town, but his name is William Berger," Chief Turner said, loud enough for everyone to hear.

"William Berger owned the Pug," Mason said.

Why I was stunned to learn the dog belonged to the deceased man I couldn't say. Was I thinking he didn't look like someone who would pick a Pug for his pet? "I'll call you back," I said.

"Hey, your friend, Rick Ziegler, hasn't reported his robbery yet," he was saying as I hung up. I walked around the counter and reached my arms out for the dog. Rapid-fire looks were going from Dana to Shelby to Mason, then back again.

"But no one calls him that," Shelby said. "Billy. Billy B. That's the waiter-singer's name, isn't it? The dog belongs, uh, belonged to the man I found dead at your house?"

I nodded that it was true.

"They know him at the vet clinic. They have all his medical records," Mason said, almost whispering.

"So they know the dog's name?" Dana squealed. "Tell us!"

"It's Wags," he said.

Joey, our second groomer, came into the lobby from the hallway, and he and Mason made eye contact.

Mason cleared his throat and coughed, then went on. "He's up-to-date on all his vaccinations except Bordetella."

"If you take him back, can they give him that one? The last thing we need here is a dog with kennel cough," I said.

"Yeah, I asked and they said they would but…" Mason's voice trailed off.

"They want to be paid first?" I asked, with a chuckle. Buckingham's was responsible for ending Dr. Walton's boarding business because of our higher level of service. And last year he ran Lady Anthea and me off the road in a drunken rage for which he was sentenced a hundred hours of community service. I shifted Wags to one arm and took a few twenty-dollar bills out of the top drawer and handed them to Mason.

"Petty cash, literally?" Mason said. He pulled a note-size piece of paper out of his pocket. "Here's the phone number and address that were stored on the chip."

The phone on the desk rang and Shelby reached for it. "It's Ass Glass," she said after looking at the caller ID.

"I think it's Class Glass," I said.

She answered the call, described what needed to be replaced, and gave him the size of the doors. We watched and waited as she made faces at the phone. We didn't know exactly what Mr. Class Glass was saying, but we were starting to feel sorry for him.

"No, no, no, no," Shelby began. "There's no need for plywood. Replace the glass. No, you do not need to *measure* the doors since I just gave you the *measurements*." She pulled out the two words to show they had the same root. "Now when can we expect you and the new glass?"

This time his answer satisfied her and she hung up.

"Way to go, Shelby. You kicked his glass," Dana said.

"His glass was grass," Mason added.

I put Wags in Mason's arms. "Joey, go with him." The laugh over Class Glass helped but Mason was taking this hard, and it didn't take a psychologist to know he would want to be with someone he cared for. Even if the two of them hadn't been a couple, Joey was a gentle soul who could make anyone feel better.

I unfolded the note. "He lives in Lewes and has a local phone number. Shelby, neither Billy B. nor that dog has ever been here, right?" I asked, stuffing the note into a pocket.

She shook her head. "Nope, but to be on the safe side I'll do a search of our database."

"Can you guys give me a ride to school?" Dana said. Cape Henlopen High was about a mile down Savannah Road.

"Sure," both Mason and Joey said.

As they were leaving they passed Rick Ziegler bringing in a cooler with our supply of raw dog food, and held the doors open for him. I'd hardly thought any more about the stolen dog food, other than to wonder if the thief was the dead man or his murderer. Shelby had inventoried what we had left. It was mostly puppy food that had been stolen.

His girlfriend, local pet photographer Dayle Thomas, was behind him. "Look who I have helping me get caught up," he said, beaming at her.

"In exchange for lunch," Dayle said.

"The lunch is to celebrate your final chemo treatment," Rick reminded her. She wore a maroon paisley scarf tied at the back of her neck.

"Rick, what she lacks in hair you make up for," Shelby said. Rick's long ponytail hung out the back of his baseball cap.

Rick and I transferred the dog food to the refrigerator in our storeroom, while Shelby told Dayle about Wags and the dead body in my driveway and how the two were connected. Rick headed back to his truck for a second cooler. "Wait, Shelby, you found a dead body?" Dayle shrieked.

Shelby nodded her head. "Sure did."

"I've got to keep unloading. Dayle, honey, get all the details."

"Did you know we had two employees here when we were robbed?" Shelby asked.

"No! That's terrible." Dayle said. "Was anyone hurt?"

"One of them is very dramatic and to hear her tell it they were almost asphyxiated by the fumes from his car. It was tiny, like a clown car and really old and—"

"Rick, that sounds exactly like your father's car," Dayle said. Then to Shelby, with a laugh, "Was the paint so rusted you couldn't tell what color the car was?"

I saw Rick pause on his way to the door. He seemed to sway.

"What's the matter, Rick?" Shelby had seen it, too.

"Uh, nothing," he said and started walking again to the door.

I was standing in the hallway, outside the kitchen, listening to the exchange and watching Rick's back as he went out the first set of doors then the outer pair. The bit of information my brain had been trying to retrieve was right there. Rick's father was the owner of Mozart's, the German deli where Billy B. had worked.

Rick's father's car had been involved in our theft. Had it been used to rob Raw-k & Roll? Several ugly thoughts raced around inside my head.

I saw someone standing outside talking to Rick, who was nodding. It was Chief Turner. I had to get to the reception desk before he came in.

"Don't mention the car," I whispered to Dayle.

She grabbed my arm. Hard. Those bony fingers were going to leave a mark. "Are you saying the dead man is Rick's father?"

"No!" Shelby and I said at the same time.

"It was his employee," I whispered.

I checked over my shoulder and Chief Turner was coming in.

Chapter 8

"I have some photos of different models of cars." Chief Turner motioned to the notebook he held.

I looked over his shoulder. Rick was still outside and on his phone. Suddenly he crammed it into his jacket pocket and looked up at the sky.

"Would you and Shelby take a look at them and tell me if one looks like the car you saw leaving here this morning, and at your house?" Chief Turner asked. "When the part-timers come in again, maybe they can look at it, too?"

Rick came in and stood behind him motionless, like a hunting dog on point. In classical point position, he was looking at the back of Chief Turner's head like it was the source of the strongest scent. I half expected his forward foot to lift. I couldn't see Dayle's face but I could tell she was frozen to the spot where she stood. I knew her to be handicapped by personal honesty and a conscience so I hoped she wouldn't pass out from the stress of this small, temporary deception I was asking of her.

Shelby reached for the book. "Can we look at this and call you later?"

Chief Turner turned to glance at me, then around the room, just then sensing the sea of tension he had entered. He returned his gaze to me. "Can we talk?"

Without waiting for an answer, he walked behind the reception desk, turning sideways to get behind Shelby, and into my office. "Chief Turner, funny story about Billy B. and my passcode." I followed him, trying to think of a way to signal to Rick that I was on his side.

From the corner of my eye I saw Shelby look at Rick. Telegraphing to him that I had this.

"Who's Billy B.?" the chief asked.

"That's what everybody calls Billy Berger. You know, William Berger."

We were in my office and I sat behind my desk while he paced. "I'm waiting for that funny story about your passcode," he said.

I gave him Dana's theory about Billy B. correctly guessing my passcode.

He stopped and shook his head in slow motion. "Okay, but there's still some connection to you. He was at your house and he broke into your business. You're sure you don't know him outside of seeing him at the deli?"

"I'm sure," I said.

He was back to pacing. "Even after you change that combination you should block the keypad with your remote or from the inside. And please remember to lock your front door." He turned and saw the expression on my face. "I don't care if this is Lewes."

"I'm not going to let you scare me. This town is my home."

He took a seat on the white leather sofa, finally, at the end closest to the desk, so he could face me. "I just want you to be safe." A throw pillow with a hound dog Elvis impersonator caught his eye, and he smiled in spite of himself. He leaned forward and put his elbows on his knees, then he sighed and waited for me to speak.

Finally I did. "You heard that the dog from the lighthouse belonged to Billy B.?"

"No! You hung up on me." He was standing again.

"He had a microchip." I caught the bewilderment in his eyes, that look he got whenever anything having to do with a dog was brought up, and said, "It's a radio-frequency device you can have implanted in your dog. Most vets and animal shelters have scanners they use to get the microchip ID number, which they call in to the pet recovery service." I handed him the piece of paper from my pocket. "Here's Billy B.'s phone number and address. I'll keep the dog until you reach his family."

"I want to find that *car*! That's the key to this case."

That, I knew, was just a matter of time, and would lead him to Rick and his father.

"Remember our last murder—"

"My last murder," he corrected.

"Whatever. You latched on to theories right away. You might be doing that again."

"I'm decisive."

"I'm not *indecisive*," I countered.

"It took you thirty-five years to decide where to live." The look on his face told me he regretted saying that as soon as it was out of his mouth.

I tried to speak, but nothing came out. I couldn't argue with what he'd said, because it was true. Instead I wanted to argue with his right to know it.

He put his hands on my desk and leaned toward me. "In law enforcement—real law enforcement—only rookies believe in coincidences. That's all I'm saying." He straightened.

"Have you forwarded the photos to me yet? Maybe I can pick up the number off the plate."

I took out my phone and scrolled to the worst, grainiest image I could find and emailed it to him.

"If you think of anything I need to know, give me a call." He hesitated then tapped his front pocket, which held his phone. "I'll blow this up and call DMV. By the time I get back to the station Marie might've found Mr. Berger's next of kin."

"I need time," I said.

"Huh?"

Damn. I'd said that out loud. "I said I'll be glad when Lady Anthea gets here." I needed her confidence and nerve.

With a parting admonition not to tell anyone the identity of Mr. Berger, a dagger to my conscience, he was gone.

Chapter 9

On his way out Chief Turner reminded Rick, again, to report his theft to the Milton police department, then he was gone. No one spoke until the last door had closed.

Dayle spoke first, "He can't find his father."

He looked down at the floor, the way a worried man does, which made Dayle start rubbing his back, drawing comforting circles, the way a woman in love does.

"So when I saw you calling someone it wasn't the Milton police? It was your father?"

Rick exhaled. "He's not answering." He gave the phone in his hand a disgusted look. "Shit. What has that crazy old fool done now?"

Dayle, Shelby, and I looked back and forth at one another. Finally I started laughing. I knew that was inappropriate but I couldn't help it. "Rick, you drink all day so you can surf sober."

"You invented the *One Evil Beer in Every Case* theory," Shelby added.

"But it's true," Rick said. "You're feeling fine, the brews are going down smoothly, then, after that *particular* can, you're a mess. How else would you explain it?"

"It's not exactly a phenomenon, sweetie," Dayle said, laughing and wrapping an arm around his waist.

"We're just saying that for you to call someone a crazy, old fool is pretty rich," I said. "Remember the night it took us half an hour to convince you that it was *not* Abraham Lincoln who said 'Friends, Romans, Countrymen lend me your ears'?"

"I'm still not completely convinced. Who did say it?"

I shrugged my shoulders. "Beats me."

"Ask Lady Anthea. She'll be here tomorrow," Shelby said.

"I'll do that!" Rick took a deep inhale. "Sue, did you tell Chief Turner that was Pop's car?"

"No! First, we don't know for certain that it was your father's car. Next, your father didn't steal that dog food or kill one of his employees!"

Rick's face did this slow transition from one emotion to the next. "I know he wouldn't kill anyone." Then he made a sound referred to in books as a chortle. "I can say with confidence he would never *intentionally* kill anyone."

"The guy who was murdered in front of Sue's house was intentionally killed," Shelby assured him.

Rick smacked the countertop, with, I would have to say, force. "Wait! Sue, did you say *kill his employee*?"

"Oh, that's right," Dayle said. "You were outside when they told me."

"You mean when we didn't tell you," Shelby corrected.

"It was Billy B. that was murdered," I said. "I'm sorry. It's hard to imagine the deli without him there singing opera."

Rick took one step back and then another. Dayle's arm was left in midair. "Billy B.?" he said, shaking his head in disbelief.

"I'm sorry," I said again.

"Dad's really going to go off the deep end. Billy B. had a way of getting him back on track when he had one of his crazy ideas." He hesitated and then gave a sad smile. "Like the time he wanted to have a drive-thru built onto the front of Mozart's."

I laughed out loud. "On Second Street?"

"Yeah. Can you imagine?" Rick said.

"No, I can't," I said. "Traffic is almost at a standstill on Second Street during the season, and pretty heavy year-round."

"I told him the city would never approve it, and that ended it, but it was the first and, as far as I know, the only time he and Billy B. ever argued. I've got to find him." He pulled his cell phone out of his jeans pocket and dialed, then sighed. "Went straight to voice mail."

"Rick, getting back to something you said, has your father ever *unintentionally* killed anyone?" I asked.

"He's come close a few times. He has one crazy scheme after another— always has. All my life. Look, Sue, I'll reimburse you for the dog food."

"Let's wait and see if he stole it," I said.

"The car you described does sound like his and he would never let anyone else drive The Bentley," Rick said. "I can tell you that much!"

"Hold on," Shelby said. "That was *not* a Bentley."

"Whoa," I said. Even I knew that.

"That's just what he would tell women to be sure they didn't cancel dates with him."

Shelby, Dayle, and I propped our heads on our elbows on the counter, ready to listen. "After my mom died, he would talk women, more like pressure or guilt them, into going out with him but they would usually cancel as soon as they could get away. He started telling them that he would pick them up in his Bentley and his success rate went up."

Dayle stared. "So women started going out with him?"

"Oh, hell, no. The percentage that canceled dropped, but as far as I know no one would get in that old heap."

"The deli is always busy, and in the summer I've seen tourists lined up outside, so why does he drive that thing?" I asked. "He could afford a new car."

"He's just different," Rick said stretching out each of the three words. He seemed about to say more but stopped and shook his head, then he put his hand on the back of Dayle's neck, drawing her to him. "Sweetie, we need to finish the deliveries."

They headed for the door, holding hands. "Sue, thanks for, uh, not telling Chief Turner everything you know," Rick called over his shoulder.

"I'm afraid all that did was buy a little time," I said. I watched the doors close and wondered what the cost to me would be. Had I just sold any chance I had of a relationship with John? Did I want to date him?

I wanted to be outside and I needed time to think and to feel.

"Shelby, when is the glass person coming?"

"He's here now," she called back. "That's his truck in the parking lot."

I looked to where she was pointing. Sure enough, a man was walking through our parking lot, carrying two panes of glass. Since it was February, the sky was already turning pink and I thought about the "red sky at night" line. It probably held for paddle boarders and surfers, too.

"Will you be okay if I leave for a while?" I asked.

"Sure," she said. "I recognize that look on your face."

I walked Abby home. So that I can run quick errands from work, I usually drive the Jeep over, but today I had walked. I couldn't drive over the spot where Billy B. had died. Not that I planned to be a pedestrian the rest of my life, I just needed a little time to pass.

The yellow crime scene tape had been taken away and the house felt *mine* again.

I changed into my wetsuit and then I loaded my paddleboard, in its board bag, onto the top of the Jeep. I tossed a towel, my personal floatation device, my paddle, and a deck bag in the back and headed out.

Five minutes later I was parked at Lewes Beach, putting on water booties, and pulling on the PFD. A few minutes after that I was in the water stand-up paddling. I had attached a suction light onto the bottom of my board and I was floating in a pool of light. I felt like I was standing on the ocean itself.

The leash connecting my ankle to the board had me feeling more grounded than I had since Shelby's call telling me that a dead body was lying in my driveway.

What did I know about Billy B.? He was just as much a part of Lewes as the Buckingham Pet Palace. Maybe more since he had been around longer. I had never had a real conversation with him. Just like everyone I knew, I had thanked him for his singing and that was all. I pulled my paddle through the water and imagined him as he sang. He had a faraway look on his face as his beautiful music filled the deli. When customers applauded, he would come out of his intense concentration and look around shyly. He made people happy for a living. Yet, someone had killed him. Why had he come to my home?

"Sue!" a woman's voice called.

I looked at the ocean surrounding me for the source. It was Charlie, with her husband, Jerry, on their SUPs. They were headed my way and I waved.

"We heard about that guy who sings German opera getting killed," Jerry said.

"And he was found by your garage door?" Charlie asked, the excitement showing in her friendly voice.

"His name was Billy B.," I said.

They nodded. "I guess I knew that at some time," Jerry said. "It'll be weird to go to Mozart's and not see him there."

"The only opera I ever heard was from him," Charlie said, with a laugh. She was looking down at the water, paddling to stay in place.

"Me, too." I started thinking about how much I wanted Chief Turner to find his relatives.

I was only vaguely aware that Jerry was telling a joke. It had to do with a woman going to the dentist and grabbing his family jewels as soon as she was in the chair. The punchline was something like the patient saying, "So we're not going to hurt one another, are we?" I laughed and brought my attention back to where it should have been, especially on the water.

"Where's Rick?" Charlie was saying. "He said he was coming out."

"I wonder if we're ever going to get Dayle on a paddleboard or a surfboard?" I asked.

I looked at the shore and saw a Lewes police car driving out of the parking lot. The line, "So *we're not going to hurt one another, are we?*" played in my head.

Chapter 10

Ordinarily when someone in law enforcement looks at me with a self-satisfied grin like the one Chief Turner was wearing on Tuesday, it meant I was about to get another ticket. Since Shelby and I were standing behind the Buckingham reception desk that was obviously not the case. He had slapped a folder down on the counter.

"I can tell there's something in there you're proud of," I said.

He shrugged and twisted around to see what Charles Andrews's Dachshund, So-Long, was rooting for behind the leg of the bench placed beneath Lady Anthea's portrait. "What's that one doing?" he asked.

"He's foraging for dog food left over from what happened yesterday morning," Shelby answered.

"Uh, uh." I had tried to interrupt her but had jumped in a beat too late.

Out of all the crabby, complaining, attention-seeking eighty-year-olds in the world, Lewes just had to have one with decent hearing.

He called to us from across the room where he was giving Joey, our second groomer, his exact instructions on how So-Long was to be groomed, spoken to, looked at, and, as I had once added in a staff meeting, we had to laugh at the dog's jokes. And Dachshunds don't have that keen a sense of humor. "Not everyone can have the housekeeping standards my wife had," Mr. Andrews said. He had been a widower since before Buckingham's opened. I'd never met the woman but she had my condolences.

I stole a sideways glance at Shelby. "Are we getting off that easy?" I whispered.

"What happened here yesterday morning?" Mr. Andrews demanded.

Nope, we weren't.

"We had a break-in," I said, as gently and apologetically as I could.

"What?!" He charged over to the dog and scooped him up like the robber was still on the premises and had an enthusiasm for small black and brown dogs.

"Everything's under control, Mr. Andrews," John said. He gave me a slow smile and gently pulled the manila folder back to hide it from the older man. "Nothing to worry about."

Then he tilted his head toward my office. I turned that way and he came around the reception desk to follow.

I sat behind my desk and he sat in the chair reserved for anyone who might want to talk to me, before tossing the folder onto the desk.

I opened it and asked, "Is there really nothing to worry about?"

He leaned forward and lowered an eyebrow. "*Are* you worried? You slept like a baby last night."

"How would you know how I slept?" Involuntarily my eyes darted to the door, then to each wall. I willed myself not to look out the window behind my desk.

"I drove through your neighborhood." He was speaking slowly, the way you talked to an animal you were afraid would bolt. I had been drawn to his baritone voice from the first time I met him, and now the measured cadence he was using calmed me, in spite of myself.

It was true that I had slept straight through until it was time to get up for my five o'clock beach run, but wasn't that for me and Abby to know?

He cleared his throat. "Shelby's statement and yours are in there. You'll see where you need to sign." We had taken turns yesterday going to the police station, about three miles away in downtown Lewes, to give said statements. "Plus a few photos from the traffic cam I think you'll find interesting. The techs really came through." He was warming to his topic, because it was tech-related. "They cleared the images up and, even with low lighting, we can make out a face."

I moved the statements aside and studied the photos. "Billy B.," I said when I saw the man with hollow cheeks and an insignificant mouth through the windshield of the old car. "Why did you do this?" I ran a finger over his face, then I picked up my statement and signed it.

"I couldn't get enough numbers off the license tag from the traffic cam or from your photos. Taylor identified the make. It was a Renault R8 from the early sixties. Mr. Berger didn't have a car registered in Delaware, but I doubt there's more than a few in the state, so we should know who it belongs to by this afternoon. It could be his but registered to a family member."

"Have you reached anyone in his family to notify?"

John shook his head. "Mr. Ziegler, the owner of Mozart's, didn't show up for work yesterday. No one's heard from him. He has a number of longtime workers and they opened up the deli." He stopped talking and studied my face. "Ziegler? Is he related to Rick Ziegler?"

I nodded. "That's his father."

"And Rick was here yesterday talking to you."

I didn't answer. I could have reminded him that Rick was delivering the raw dog food, but when the truth came out, the dodge would just embarrass both of us.

"Is there anything else you're not telling me?"

Technically, the twenty-four hours Rick asked me for had expired but I had wanted some kind of go-ahead from him before I talked to Chief Turner. "Rick's father didn't come into work this morning, either?" I asked.

"No."

"You checked his house?"

"He lives above the store and hasn't been home as far as we can tell."

"The car's his," I said.

John was back to being Chief Turner. "He's probably the murderer."

"That's exactly what I was afraid you'd say!" I said, and my shoulders slumped.

"I *am* going to bring him in for questioning for the murder of his employee. A possible scenario is that the victim stole the car, committed a crime, and Ziegler killed him and took his car back." He jumped up so violently that he almost took the chair with him, and I cracked up laughing.

"Sorry," I said, wiping my eyes.

He turned back around and moved the chair off his thigh. He was laughing, too. "I can't stay mad at you," he said.

"You give it a pretty good try," I reminded him.

"Does Rick know where his father is?" he asked.

"No, and he's worried."

"If I can talk to him, he might be able to tell me who the victim's emergency contact is."

"I know," I said, nodding.

He turned and went back to the lobby. I picked up Shelby's statement and followed him out.

Charles Andrews was gone and Joey had taken So-Long to the grooming suite in the back.

Chief Turner pointed at Lady Anthea's portrait. "She's flying in today, right?"

"She's here!"

Actually it sounded like Lady Anthea had said, "She's *heah*."

Shelby ran around the counter to hug Buckingham's co-owner while I called Mason and Joey on the intercom.

"What a difference a few months makes," I said to Chief Turner. He chuckled and nodded. He knew all about our rocky initial meeting.

Since our partnership agreement had been negotiated and accomplished with emails, our first in-person meeting had been the week of the Pet Parents Appreciation Gala. Between the signing of the contract and that week she had given us lots of support—use of her name, use of the name of her estate, Frithsden, and photographs galore. Her family estate was grand and the gardens were dramatic. Using her guidance we'd achieved our own elegance at Buckingham's with golf-course-green and burgundy walls and dark wood furniture. She hadn't stopped there. She'd emailed us regularly and it was what was in *those* missives that had caused us to dread meeting her.

"Did I tell you about the time she compared me to someone named Bia because of the hours I worked?" I whispered to Chief Turner. "Who would know that Bia was the Greek goddess of force and raw energy without Googling it?"

"Not me," he said.

"She was the sister of Nike, who we *did* know, but only as running shoes."

"Greek mythology, huh?"

"Sometimes Roman, but not just gods and goddesses. She brings up people in operas, famous paintings, composers..." I trailed off when I heard my groomers getting closer.

Mason and Joey ran into the lobby and I waited to see if they would continue their tradition that made Lady Anthea giggle, every time. They stopped in front of her and slowly bowed.

She clapped her hands and laughed. Someone not upper class, someone whose grandmother wasn't lady-in-waiting to the queen, might have called the guys cheeky. "It's marvelous to be back here. Now, where is Sue?"

The front doors opened and two men I didn't know walked in and edged past the group in the middle of the lobby. Both wore black slacks, silk ties, and white shirts starched so stiff I could hardly take my eyes off them. The older man held a leash for a well-behaved Airedale Terrier. The dog was sedate so surely Chief Turner wouldn't be bothered by *him*. Shelby started to greet the pair but I told her that I would take care of them.

"Good afternoon," I said.

They skirted around the laughing, talking group and made their way to me. "We'll catch up later," I called to Lady Anthea.

"I want to hear *everything*," she said.

John was backing away and had almost made his escape when the older of the two stopped him.

"Chief," the man said with a nod. He shifted the leash to his left hand, reached out for a handshake. "Good to see you again." He wore silver aviator eyeglasses on his jowly face. Thinning, white hair had been pressed into service as a comb-over, valiantly fighting the good fight.

He spoke with an accent that was pleasing to the ear and I was simultaneously trying to figure out where he was from and concentrating on keeping my mouth from imitating him. *Gwud ta seeee ya agan.*

"Likewise, Mr. Fourie," John said, shaking the man's wide, square hand and looking slightly bored.

Fourie? Where had I heard that name? He was Mr. Edutainer! I chanced a look over his shoulder at my employees. Or as we liked to say, "Heeeeere's Mr. Edutaaaaaaainer." Why had no one told me he was bringing his dog here?

"Please call me Howard. And this is my son, David." His gravelly voice trailed off at the end of the sentence, as he turned to where he thought his son was standing. No son. Or rather, the son had drifted off to the gift store section of our lobby, and was trying to place a call on his cell phone. He turned his attention to me. After running his eyes up and down as much of me as he could see, he said, "Sweetheart, I'm dropping my dog off for grooming."

"You're Mr. Fourie?" I asked.

He nodded and smirked.

"You had a phone call. The nineteen seventies called. They want their sexist language back."

The father's mouth dropped open, as did John's. Mason, Joey, Shelby, and Lady Anthea all sucked in their breath, their eyes wide, as they hungrily waited to see how this would play out, like I had opened a bag of treats in the middle of the puppy play room. I don't work twelve hours a day to be spoken to like that. Suddenly the son bellowed out a laugh, and the spell was broken.

"I like it," Mr. Fourie called out. I had no idea what he liked.

"I'm Sue Patrick, one of the owners of Buckingham's."

Shelby came around and started clicking the keypad. "We received Ariadne's—uh, am I pronouncing her name correctly?"

Howard Fourie nodded, yes.

Shelby continued, "We have her vaccination records from your vet in South Africa." Oh, yeah, South Africa. That was the accent. "She'll be with our lead groomer today."

Mason had come up to greet the dog and take the leash. "Well, you've come a long way," he said to the dog.

David Fourie rejoined us. "We're organizing the anniversary celebration of finding the eighteenth-century artifacts from the shipwreck in Roosevelt Inlet." The younger man was just as corporate as his father. He had slimmer hips and more narrow shoulders. His hair was black and thick, on the longish end of the spectrum. He looked like he was in his mid-twenties. So why was he talking like a fifty-year-old? Only his small mouth looked like his dad's, and he spoke like him. I wondered why I had thought the resemblance was stronger when they came in, and then realized it was because they walked with the same gait, that is, confidence bordering on swagger.

"Interesting," Mason said, so professionally the guy never even suspected the sarcasm loaded into the response. He had one of our leashes lassoed around his shoulder and pulled it off of himself and onto the dog in one fluid motion. "We'll telephone when we're done." He handed David their leash back, which he'd removed.

With that, he, Joey, and Ariadne walked down the hall to the grooming suite. David Fourie's phone rang and he returned to the side of the lobby.

As he walked away, I heard him say, "Have you secured funding? The city council meets this week."

Chief Turner and Lady Anthea were standing in front of the reception desk. "Good to see you again," he said, smiling at Lady Anthea.

She looked down the hallway after Mason and Joey. "With a welcome like that, I now know how Elvis must have felt."

She laughed and they went on to talk about jet lag, the weather, what Lewes was like in the off-season until her accent attracted Howard Fourie's attention. He had been listening in and he turned to me. "Who's that?"

"Let me introduce you." I moved down to the end of the counter. "Mr. Fourie, this is Lady Anthea Fitzwalter, the co-owner of Buckingham's." They shook hands while her title sunk in. What I'd overheard of the son's phone conversation reminded me of some work needed in our store. I sauntered off to do some critical and urgent shelf restocking.

"A pleasure to meet you," Lady Anthea said behind me.

"The pleasure's all mine," he returned. "You've just arrived?"

"Yes, just today," she said.

"Same as my son." He nodded in our direction. "Just flew in."

"I heard Shelby say your dog is named Ariadne. Are you a fellow opera devotee?"

As David's back was turned I lowered myself behind a display case of life-size inflatable dogs, wishing I hadn't seen that exasperated look on John's face. I could have done without the eye roll, too.

The father hadn't answered Lady Anthea's simple question. Suddenly what I wasn't hearing was just as interesting as what I was listening to with David. I didn't understand the beat the father took to say if he liked opera or not. She could ask me that question any time.

The son spoke again and I brought my attention back to why I was kneeling on the floor in the first place. "We'll bring any of the more noteworthy items back to South Africa where they belong, anything significant." There was a pause, then he said, "Sure, including the section of the wine bottle with the logo."

His voice registered a bit higher than his father's, but that's not what had stopped the pretend-straightening of the blow-up Pugs I was doing. The bottom of the wine bottle that was found was from the oldest winery in *South Africa* and it's still in operation today.

"It won't be a problem with these people," the younger Fourie said. "We've collab'd with the city on their little celebration which has greased the way for that."

Collab'd? What the hell? Ohhhh, they have *collaborated* with Lewes.

I heard the doors open and close and looked to my side since I'd hate for some conscientious bloodhound to sneak up on me. It was John, and he was leaving.

Back in the open section of the lobby, Lady Anthea rescued the Fourie she was with after his second "ub, ub," on that tricky opera question. She said, "I'm here to give morning dog trick classes and then an agility class in the afternoon."

The elder Fourie said, "Hmm." Before saying to Shelby, "Sign my dog up for this week's classes. What did you say it was—tricks?"

"A pet parent has to accompany the dog. Someone as busy as you might not have time," Lady Anthea demurred.

"That won't be a problem," Howard said.

At the same time Shelby was saying, "I'm sorry, both morning and afternoon classes are filled to capacity and we have a waiting list."

I jumped up from the floor. "It's okay. Arianna, Adriana, Adriadne can have Abby's spot."

Chapter 11

Since my cover was blown, I went back to the group at the reception desk.

Howard Fourie nodded, his substitute for thanking me for making room for his dog to be a part of Lady Anthea's class.

"Sue and Lady Anthea, my son and I are hosting a little dinner at the Gate House restaurant tomorrow evening, and we'd like you to join us," he said, looking at Lady Anthea, then me, then back again. The way he had puffed up prior to extending the invitation made me think that by little dinner, he meant, big dinner.

I sensed that Lady Anthea was about to turn him down, so I had to act fast. "Sounds fun." By that I meant the opposite. "We'd love to. Shelby, are you free?"

Fourie, the elder, gulped.

"I really should handle closing tomorrow night," she said, giving me a look that said, *I know what you're doing and thanks but no thanks.*

"I've reserved the Gate House for the evening," said Howard, relieved and wheeling around to leave. "Do you know where that is?"

I nodded. "Yes, it's very nice."

David was following his father out and said over his shoulder, "Lewes has more than its fair share of elegant restaurants."

I was pathetically and illogically thinking better of him after his compliment to my city, as I walked around the desk on the way to my office.

Lady Anthea and Shelby stood like statues, eyes glued to the doors. As soon as the men reached the pavement outside, Lady Anthea began, "I want to hear all about the murder!"

"We have to start with the robbery!" Shelby said.

They followed me back to my office. My cell phone was lit up because I had not one but two texts. I read them while Shelby, starting from the beginning, told Lady Anthea all that had happened since yesterday morning. The first text was from John Turner, who wanted me to go to dinner Wednesday night. *Sorry, I have to work late.*

I went on to the second text. "Thank goodness!" I yelled.

Both women turned to me. "Rick found his father!"

"I was just getting to Rick's father's part in all this," Shelby said and sat on the sofa.

"He's taking him to talk to Chief Turner and he wants me to go along." I looked at the clock on my phone. "They're meeting in half an hour," I said, as I typed. "I'm telling him I'll be there."

Lady Anthea sat next to Shelby and seemed to relish all the details. While they talked I printed the roster for the Trick and Agility classes. At the end I handed the papers to Lady Anthea. She scanned them and then looked at me, with what one of my mysteries—I believe it was *The Green, Green Grass over the Grave*—called a gimlet eye. "Now tell me why you added Howard Fourie's dog to my already full class!"

"I want to keep an eye on those men," I said. "I think he's trying to take a very, very old, rare and valuable artifact discovered on Lewes Beach out of the country." I told them what I had heard David Fourie say.

Lady Anthea clapped her hands. "Very old artifact? How old? Fifteenth century? Sixteenth century?"

"Uh, nooooo," I said. "The ship sank in 1774."

"That's not old," she said.

"It is to us," I said, standing up for our country.

"How valuable? And what type of relic is it? A tool or maybe jewelry?"

"Well, see, there's this winery in South Africa named Groot Constantia Estate and Winery. And a British ship, the *Severn*, was carrying some wine made there," I said.

"Lewes has a bottle of wine from the eighteenth century! That is remarkable!" Shelby and I tried to interrupt Lady Anthea but she was getting excited. "Or are you saying the town has a case…"

Finally, Shelby touched her arm. "It's just the bottom of a wine bottle."

"What?" Lady Anthea was incredulous. "What makes it rare? Was that all that remained of the ship's cargo?"

"Uh, not exactly," Shelby said. "There were about fifty-six thousand pieces. When the US Army Corp of Engineers dredged the bay people starting finding artifacts washed up onto Lewes Beach. There were some buttons, pipes, and buckles for shoes…"

"Lewes has fifty-six thousand pieces in its museum?" she asked, back to being enthralled.

"No, most of it went to the Delaware state archives," I said.

"To protect the bottom of a bottle you overfilled my training class?" she asked. "The bottom of a wine bottle is not exactly the Temple of Dendur."

"Plus, I have us going to dinner with a bunch of corporate stiffs," I admitted. "I'm sharing the pain."

"Easy now," Shelby said. "That's what my husband used to be." She paused before starting again. "I'd like to make a suggestion. After the dinner, let protecting the artifact go and concentrate on the murder. That's much more important."

"Ahhh," I said. I had just figured out why John had that expression on his face when he saw me eavesdropping on David Fourie. "Chief Turner thinks this will keep me busy and I'll leave Billy B.'s murder investigation to him."

"I'm not keen on disagreeing with you, Shelby, but maybe we should investigate what the Fouries are up to, rather than the murder," Lady Anthea said. "It's obvious Rick Ziegler's father is involved. If he's not the murderer, he might be an accomplice. And Rick might be asking you to help his father get away with a crime."

I was shaking my head. "I don't think he killed that man."

"Because you think Rick's a great guy?" Shelby asked.

I squirmed since I'd never even met his father, and finally admitted, "Yeah, maybe. I don't know. It doesn't seem like someone with a son like Rick could be a murderer."

"I understand that Rick is a free spirit, but your reasoning would hardly stand up in court," Lady Anthea said. "One scenario is that this Billy B. individual stole the automobile from Mr. Ziegler. Another is that the car owner let Billy B. use his car to come and break in to Buckingham's. Neither option is pleasant. Have you considered that?"

"I don't know enough to consider anything." I shrugged my shoulders and stood. "I better get going if I'm going to meet Rick at the police station. I'll know more after I hear what he has to say. I understand if you don't want to go with me. Would you rather stay here and begin setting up for your class?"

"No, I had better accompany you," Lady Anthea said, getting up from the sofa.

Shelby said, "Good! Protect her from herself."

"Protecting Chief Turner from her is what I had in mind," Lady Anthea said and we promenaded out.

Chapter 12

I had texted Rick that we were on our way and he was waiting for us by the curb, with a grayer and wider version of himself. I knew Rick to be somewhere in his thirties and his father looked to be late-fifty-ish. His hair and stubble were about thirty-seventy black and silver. They turned in tandem to watch us park the Jeep and that's when I saw just how different the two men were. Rick's movements were decisive, almost hyper. Whereas his dad seemed to move in molasses.

We got out and they walked to meet us.

When they were closer, Lady Anthea leaned near my shoulder and whispered, "Good Lord, if he was a dog I'd say he had the mange."

I took in the gray tint to the older man's complexion. With the image her words had planted in my brain, I doubted I'd ever be able to eat at Mozart's again. Thank you very much.

"Dad, this is Sue Patrick, a friend of mine," Rick said. "Thanks for coming," he added in a whisper. He lowered his eyebrows and seemed to be trying to send me a message. He looked stressed and exasperated. I had never, ever seen Rick in either of those states before. I take that back. When Dayle broke up with him while she was undergoing chemo, he was desperately unhappy.

I held out my hand to shake his father's. "Mr. Ziegler," I began, since Rick hadn't told me his father's first name, "nice to meet you. This is Lady Anthea, my business partner." He shook my hand and then hers.

"We don't often get royalty around here," he said.

"Oh, I'm not royalty," she said.

"Sue," a baritone voice called out. "A word please."

"No," I said.

Without missing a beat, John, though he was in full Chief Turner mode, said, "No? That's not the word I had in mind." He turned to the Ziegler men. "Let's go in."

He led us through the small lobby and down a hallway. Midway down he stopped and held up a hand for Lady Anthea, Rick, and me to halt. "Mr. Ziegler, do you have an attorney?"

"No, I don't need one. When did getting your classic automobile stolen become a crime in this town?"

Rick cringed at his father's description of his car.

"You three can wait in the lobby," John said. He turned on his heel and opened the door for Rick's dad to go into the room and followed him. The uniformed Lewes police officer, a young woman I'd last seen when my business and then my home both became crime scenes, went into the interrogation room after them. The door was closed on our civilian faces and we stood there glaring at it like it had used bad language then slammed shut.

"This is not going to go well," Rick said, still staring at the wooden door.

"I've had a long day," Lady Anthea said. "Can we sit in the lobby?"

"Sure," Rick said. "I forgot you flew in today. Would you like some coffee? Or tea, maybe?"

"No, just a place to sit."

We sank onto a vinyl sofa and looked longingly at the door to the interrogation room.

"Did Dayle have a doctor's appointment? Is that why you asked me to come?" I asked.

"No, she's done with those. Hopefully forever." He paused and took a breath. "Actually, I was hoping you could use your influence with the police chief," he said.

"I don't know if I have any."

Lady Anthea snorted a laugh.

I rolled my eyes and changed the subject. "Don't forget Mason and Joey have something special planned for us on the beach tonight after dark. They've kept it all a big secret, but it involved trips to Walgreens and the grocery store." I turned to Rick. "You and Dayle are coming, right?"

He jerked his jaw in the direction of the door. "Depends on how things go here."

We went back to staring at the door.

"Where did you find your dad?" I asked.

"He was in his apartment, hiding out. Not answering his phone. Not even opening up when I went over there."

"Ouch," I said.

"He says I throw shade on him."

"What in the world does that mean?" Lady Anthea asked, also mesmerized by the closed door.

I had heard Dana and Mason use the term. "It means to trash someone in front of other people." I tore my eyes from the door to twist on the sofa and face Rick. "That does not sound like you."

He gave me a weak smile but before he could say anything, the door opened, and Chief Turner strode our way. He sat in the chair opposite our sofa.

"Rick, Ziggy is free to go," he announced.

"Who's Ziggy?" Rick asked.

"Your dad—he said it was what everybody called him."

"His name is Martin. No one calls him Ziggy," Rick said.

"Well, he's given us the names of the two individuals he says took the victim's dog. We'll try to find them." John opened up his notebook. "Do you know Arthur Dent or Ford Prefect?"

"No," Rick said, shaking his head, puzzled.

"I think you should let Rick and me sit in," I said, trying not to laugh.

"Why would I do that? I'm getting somewhere," John said.

"Not really." Yeah, I was gloating. "Arthur Dent and Ford Prefect are the main characters in *The Hitchhiker's Guide to the Galaxy.*"

In one fast, angry arc, Chief Turner was out of the chair and halfway back to the interrogation room. He pushed the door open. "Sit down!" we heard him say before the door closed again.

"Did you find the car?" I asked. We were speaking to one another but back to staring at that damn door.

"No," Rick said. "It wasn't at Mozart's."

"Rick, your father said it was stolen. Does *he* know where the car is?" Lady Anthea asked in a low tone, in case any of the uniformed officers who walked by from time to time were listening. "I'm not familiar with the laws here, but in England that would be classified as insurance fraud."

"Insurance?!" Rick and I practically yelled the word at the same time.

"She hasn't seen the ca—" I got out before going into uncontrollable laughter.

Rick started laughing too, and we were both wiping our eyes. I doubled over on the sofa at the thought of the insurance premiums compared to the value of Rick's father's car.

When Rick was able to, he said, "I don't know if he knows where the car is or not. You see, my father has an unusual kind of relationship with the truth."

The interrogation room door opened and I straightened up and tried to look serious. John looked happy. He sat in the same chair, and leaned forward, his elbows on his knees. "He was afraid to tell me the truth before. This is serious. What really happened was someone kidnapped the dog that was left at the lighthouse and demanded dog food as ransom. It fits in with there being two robberies." He turned to Rick. "Sue told me how expensive the good stuff is. The ringleader has a teenager working for him who was going to pass the dog food on to some other teenagers to sell."

"Did he tell you who the mastermind was?" Lady Anthea asked.

"The name's Walter White," Chief Turner said.

"It's going to be a long night," I said with a sigh.

"Please let Sue and me go in there," Rick pleaded.

Chief Turner's eyes moved from one of us to the other. "You think that's an alias?"

"He's the main character from *Breaking Bad*, a TV show," Rick said, *breaking* it to him as gently as he could.

"Son of a...!" The speed and ferocity in Chief Turner's return to the room startled me.

When I saw the door had closed all the way, I whispered, "Good one, Daddy-O."

The next time the door opened, Chief Turner leaned out. "Sue and Rick, would you come in?"

When I was close enough to him to speak in a low voice, I asked, "The last time you came out you mentioned the dog food robberies. Did Mr. Ziegler bring them up? Does he know about them?"

He had lowered his head to hear me and now he was looking into my eyes, closing the distance between our faces. Then he straightened, smashed his lips into a tight line, and shook his head. "No," he whispered.

I looked around him, back at Lady Anthea, still seated on the sofa in the lobby. She stood and motioned for me to go on ahead.

"Are you going to look for a place to get a cup of tea?" I asked.

"Put a *G* and an *and* on that and you'll hit the mark," she said.

"Huh?" Rick said, joining Chief Turner and me.

I laughed. "I'm trying to convert her from her gin and tonics to orange crushes but I haven't had much luck." I'd introduced Lady Anthea to the state drink of Delaware last year.

"When in Lewes, Lady Anthea," he called over his shoulder.

I watched as she headed for the door; again struck by how comfortable we were around her now.

Chapter 13

"Uh-oh," was how Martin Ziegler greeted us. He looked tired and it seemed almost like keeping that smirk on his face was real work. His tone had been sarcastic but he looked at Rick with affection. I'd just met him but my read was that he was glad his son was there. Of course, hell would freeze over before he would admit it.

Rick sat next to his dad and I sat across from Mr. Funny Man. Chief Turner took the chair next to me and tapped the fancy recorder in the middle of the table. "Interview is resuming. Sue Patrick and Rick Ziegler are also present."

Martin pointed a stubby finger at me. "I want the dog."

"Chill, Pop," Rick said.

"I love that pooch and I can give him a good home," he said with a sniffle, added on for maximum drama.

"What's his name?" I asked.

The beat it took him to answer was all it took for me to know my hunch was right. I've never known a pet parent to refer to their dog as the pooch. People wanting you to go out with them, buy something, or vote for their candidate said "pooch." What did Martin Ziegler want?

"It's Billy B.," he said.

"I meant the dog, the Pug. What's his name?"

"It's Puggie," he said, finally and with such assuredness that I was ready to bet good money he thought I didn't know the dog's name either.

I shook my head. "It's Wags."

The corners of his lips tilted down. For some curious reason he was disappointed that I knew.

"He'll stay with me until Billy B.'s next of kin can be contacted, but I'm curious to know why you want him."

"To give him a good home," he answered. I didn't bother to say the dog was spending his days at a five-star pet palace getting very expensive classes from Lady Anthea, gratis, and his nights being spoiled by Mason and Joey.

"Pop?" Rick's tone was stern.

"Billy B. was my employee and that's the least I can do." He stuck his chin out defiantly.

"Pop!"

"What?" Martin Ziegler yelled.

"Why do you keep saying Billy B. was your employee?"

"Why not?"

This exchange sent Chief Turner scrambling through his old-school notebook. "You must have referred to him as your employee five or six times. He's not?"

Martin leaned toward me, like we were the best of pals. "Ms. Patrick, explain to him that in a small business titles often aren't relevant." He sneered at John. "If you're not one of us, you just don't understand." He smiled and added in soulful eyes as a bonus.

"Ziggy? May I call you Ziggy?" I cooed.

"Of course. Please do," he said.

"Ziggy, would you like to take me out for a drink? Let's get out of here."

His mouth dropped open. When he recovered, he looked at Chief Turner for either assistance or permission, or both.

John raised his hands, palms up. "By all means. You're free to go."

I stood. "I'll wait out front for you to pick me up."

"Gimme ten or fifteen minutes. I'll be right back—" That's when Martin froze, his backside hovering over his chair. He realized he had pretty much admitted he had his car back, or at least knew where it was. You can't just make a direct run at someone like Mr. Ziegler and expect an honest answer. I hoped John was taking notes in his little notepad on this.

He sat down. "I told you it was stolen."

"You have the car now?" John asked.

All this got him from Martin, never-aka Ziggy, was a scowl.

Just last month I read a book about someone taking something that belonged to someone else, and that person got it back and the first person ended up dead. By "The End," we knew that the second person, that is, the owner, had killed him. The source was *Nine-Tenths of Death*. Martin Ziegler had done his damnedest to incriminate himself. And then there was Rick's question about why he was calling Billy B. his employee. What had he been? Was this just more of Martin's craziness or did his actual status in the business have anything to do with the murder? After all his stories, the only thing I knew for sure was that if Lady Anthea and I were going to find out who killed Billy B. we would have to know everything that had happened early yesterday morning. We would have to find the facts in the chaos that was the Martin Ziegler-created reality. For now, Rick had to find an off-ramp for his father.

"Did Billy B. steal your vehicle?" John was asking. Another scowl. Chief Turner pulled a folded sheet of paper out of the inside pocket of his jacket and flattened it before laying it on the table in front of Martin. "Here's a photo of the victim driving your car yesterday morning."

"He may have borrowed it," Martin answered. "He'd never steal from me."

"Do you know why he borrowed your car?" John asked.

"Maybe he couldn't figure out Uber," he said.

"Pop," Rick said, stretching the word out, his voice filled with a plea to get back on the straight and narrow.

"He went over there to get a dog to track his and find it." He looked at me. I liked the way he hadn't held my earlier deception against me. "That's what dogs do, right?"

"Only if they've been trained to," I said.

Mr. Ziegler went on, "Well, your dog is probably trained in a lot of things. And with all the dogs going in and out of Buckingham's some of them must know how to track, right?"

Sure, his theory had a crazy number of holes, but I believed there was some legit information woven in. The case had something to do with dogs, or a dog, Wags. It had not escaped my notice that he alluded to Abby. "You knew Billy B. came to my house and to Buckingham's?" I gave Rick a *this isn't good* look, and John saw it. Martin knew his car had been at my place and that Billy B. had been there, too. This closed off any possibility that the car had been abandoned somewhere and he had found it, which was flimsy but there were probably attorneys out there sleazy enough to use it. "Why would he steal from Rick and me first?" I asked.

Rick rubbed his forehead. "Pop, if you don't know, you don't know."

"So when can I get Wagner?" By changing the subject instead of making up a story, Martin was restoring my faith in humanity. He pronounced the composer's name correctly and with a German accent. *Vagner.* Why had he pretended not to know the dog's name before? I had said Wags, but few people would make that connection. Actually, Lady Anthea was the only person I knew whose brain would spring to the composer, instead of to what a dog's tail did.

"Wags. Wagner. I get it now," I said.

"Some opera singer Billy knew was going into assisted living and she gave him the dog. She used to live around here and liked his singing. That was about five or six years ago." Martin smiled at the memory.

It was a nice story but I still wanted to know why he'd led us to believe he didn't know the dog's name, and why he wanted him, though I doubted I'd find out from him.

"Martin, can I ask you another question? The whole town thought a lot of Billy B. but few of us feel like we *knew* him. Why was that?" I looked at Martin and hoped he would say something honest.

He looked at the wall over my shoulder and I saw his jaw clench. "I know what you mean. He would sing opera every day for lunch and dinner but when it came to talking about himself, no dice. I asked him once what some of those songs meant and he told me which ones were love songs and which ones were about families, or just life. But if I ever asked about where he came from he'd clam up. He did say that keeping a low profile was how you stayed safe in this life." I believed what he had said, and hoped I wouldn't be disappointed.

"Did Billy B. not have a car?" I asked.

Martin shook his head no.

"Then how did he get to work every day?" I asked.

"He walked," Martin said.

"I have his address. He would have had to walk at least four or five miles each way!" Chief Turner said.

"He liked it. Once told me his father did the same thing. His old man used to say that just getting out and walking with no one to stop you was the best feeling in the world."

Chief Turner looked unconvinced but waited before he asked, "Mr. Ziegler, do you have any idea how much trouble you are in? Even if I *forget* the misleading information you've given me here tonight, instead of adding on obstructing an investigation, and *forget* you claimed your car was stolen when you had it all along, you're looking at a murder charge."

Martin started to interrupt but Chief Turner cut him off. "The victim had possession of your car almost up until the time he was killed. Now you have the car. Where is it?"

"In the parking lot of Fowler's Beach," he said.

I didn't know if Chief Turner knew where that was, but I could tell him later that it was a few miles north of Lewes on Route 1.

John was becoming more angry and frustrated, and spoke with what I would call his last-chance voice. "I'm about to ask you a question and I want you to think carefully before you tell me another untruth. Was Billy B. alive when you retrieved your car from Sue's driveway?"

The question was so un-Chief-John-Turner that all I could do was stare. First, it was a question. I had expected a statement that began with the words, "I'm arresting you for." Second, that he hadn't jumped straight to "Did you murder William Berger?"

"He wants a lawyer," Rick said. There it was; there was his off-ramp. Now all we had to do was hope his father would stop talking, by that I mean lying, long enough to drive onto it.

Chapter 14

After Rick lawyered up his father, Chief Turner leaned back in his chair and looked at each of us. Then he glanced over at Officer Statler who had been sitting at the end of the table so quietly I had forgotten she was there. "Make arrangements to have that car brought in," he told the young woman. She gazed at him with such adoration I thought she would have gladly pulled the car up Route 1 with her bare hands. "Sue, what city is it in?"

"Milford," I said.

"Call the Milford police and let me know if there's a problem." She left the room, sidestepping behind the chairs, and John went back to sitting and glaring at us. I wondered if I could go help her, just to get out of that little room. Then I reminded myself I had practically begged to get into it.

Finally I put us out of our misery by asking, "Would you let Martin go based on Rick's assurance that his father won't leave town?"

"Rick, how does that sound to you?" John asked.

Rick nodded. I doubted he wanted to babysit his father, but it was probably the best offer he was going to get. He stood and as I watched, his father beat him through the door. "Dayle and I'll see you later, Sue," Rick called over his shoulder, with a weak smile. Then he stopped. "Now do you see why I need Dayle?" I smiled and he walked out to catch up with Martin.

I knew a few texts had come in while I'd been sitting there and since murder or no murder I still had a business to run, I pulled my phone out of my hoodie pocket. The latest one was from Lady Anthea. Mason and Joey had picked her up and they were waiting for me at Lewes Beach. I put the phone away and looked over at Chief Turner, who had resumed his sage-like position. He had pushed his chair back and his legs were stretched out about a mile and a half.

"Thank you for not locking Martin Ziegler up," I said.

He shook his head like what he had done was nothing. "He's not going anywhere with Rick and his restaurant here."

"Lewes is lucky to have you," I said.

He jerked up straight. "Is that how *you* feel?"

"Yeah. Wouldn't most police officers have locked him up after the way he made himself look guilty?"

John gave a little laugh. "He did tell some whoppers, didn't he?" Then he stared at the door through which the others had left, and said, "About Rick and Dayle, when you see that kind of love, how can you still be a cynic?"

"Is it love or need?" I asked. Rick had said *need.*

"Who cares? I don't," he said.

That was a conversation I wasn't ready for, so instead I used my standby—humor. "You're going to have to stop suspecting my friends of murder before I'll go out with you."

"Martin Ziegler's a friend of yours?" he asked, smiling.

"Well, stop suspecting family members of my friends. I'll admit Martin's an acquired taste, but there's something about him I understand." I hoped he wouldn't ask for me to elaborate, because I wasn't sure I could. Instead he sat there looking at me. Finally, I stood to leave and said, "A few of us are meeting at Lewes Beach—sort of a welcome-back party for Lady Anthea. Want to come?"

He hesitated, then said, "I'd like to but I need to stay here in case there's any problem getting that car impounded."

"Sure, I understand." I walked behind him on my way out.

Suddenly, I felt his hand wrap around my wrist and I stopped. "I'll try to stop by," he said.

* * * *

I parked the Jeep and got out. Although it wasn't quite six-thirty, it was dark on the beach. Even at night it wasn't hard to find my group of friends, which included staff, customers, surfers, and other people from around Lewes who had met Lady Anthea during her first trip to Lewes and to Buckingham's. I just followed the sound of laughing and loud talking. They were standing in a group where the parking lot ended and the sandy beach began.

"Sue! Hi!" yelled Betsy Rivard, who was a pet parent and Lewes's new mayor.

The group gathered around me and I saw several of them were holding two-liter soda bottles.

"Where's the beer? Were you afraid Chief Turner would be here?" I asked.

"You'll see," Mason said. "Lady Anthea, you stand over there." He pointed to a spot next to me.

As soon as she complied, a number of people in the group, those holding a soda bottle or two, ran down toward the ocean. I looked around to see who was left.

"What are they about?" Lady Anthea asked those that were still standing with us.

Several people chuckled but no one answered her.

"It's a surprise," I said, crossing my fingers this would work.

"Now I'm really curious," Lady Anthea said.

Rick and Dayle came to stand behind us. Dottie, her Dalmatian, was with them. "Sue, thanks for suggesting Turner let Pop go," Rick said.

I nodded. "I don't think I get any credit. That was all him."

"What are you saying?!" Dayle hissed, after a quick look around. "I remember how he was last year. Suspecting Henry's fiancée one minute, then the girlfriend the next. I was scared to death I was going to be hauled in."

From the ocean where waves were lapping up onto the beach we heard Mason yell, "One! Two! Three!"

They began shaking the soda bottles. As we watched they lit up fluorescent green. Then they held them out, some connecting end to end.

"They've written something!" Lady Anthea cried. "L. A. D. Y. A. Lady A?"

"Lady A!" they yelled.

We clapped and cheered for them. I looked over at my business partner and she was wiping her eyes. "That is the loveliest gesture," she said. "How in the world did they do that?"

I hugged her. "You mean a lot to all of us."

"These last few months have been extremely difficult. Thank heavens for the training classes," she whispered.

I knew she was referring to her brother, the duke. Privately Shelby and I called him the idiot duke. He was such a bad manager of Frithsden that Lady Anthea had to be twice as good at bringing in funds. She told me last year how much her percentage of the profits from Buckingham's had helped out. Now it looked like the money from the trick and agility classes was just in time.

I thought we would all be more comfortable if I changed the subject. "First, you leave about a fourth of some lemon lime soda in the bottle, then you add baking soda and three caps of peroxide to it. Then when you shake it you get a homemade glow stick. It was Mason's idea to hold them together to spell out Lady A."

I yelled down to the group on the beach midway between the ocean and where we stood, "We'll be right there." Then I turned so that we could huddle and Rick and I told Lady Anthea and Dayle what we'd learned in Martin's interview.

"I still have a few questions," I said.

"I can't wait to hear them," a sarcastic, baritone voice said in the dark.

I looked at Rick, but it wasn't him. He stared at Dayle, who had turned to Lady Anthea, who in turn gave me a quizzical look. Then we reversed again looking at one another. In the seconds that maneuver took us we realized exactly whose loaded-with-attitude voice was addressing us.

"Good evening, Chief Turner," I said with an eye roll.

Someone was playing the Elvis satellite station on their phone. The song was "Suspicious Minds" and I was surprised at how I could hear the music over the sound of the waves. Out there with my friends was where I wanted to be, but instead I moved to the side to let Chief Turner in to our group.

"First, what does he want with Wags?" I asked.

Rick shook his head. "No idea. He's not responsible enough to take care of a dog."

"Maybe he's lonely. You said he and Billy B. were close," Dayle offered.

"Baby, Pop cares about Pop and nobody else," Rick said with a sigh.

"Next, if Billy B. wasn't his employee, what was he?" I asked.

"I can answer that," Chief Turner said. "It's a matter of public record. He was a co-owner. They were equal partners, fifty-fifty."

"I never knew what their exact arrangement was, but I knew Billy B. had some skin in the game," Rick said.

"Now that Billy B. is dead, does your father own Mozart's solely or do Billy B.'s heirs own his half?" Lady Anthea asked.

"That's the question of the day," Chief Turner said to her.

You don't have to read as many mysteries as I do—just last week I read *The Motive for the Mister*—to know he was thinking about a motive for Billy B.'s murder, or more specifically for a good reason to charge Rick's dad.

"I don't know yet," Chief Turner continued. "We have his address. He has a condo in Plantations—"

"In Plantations or Plantations East?" I interrupted.

He shook his head, and then answered a completely different question. "No, you cannot go with us."

"If I didn't know you better, I'd think that was a hard no," I said.

"Anyway, I'm going over there in the morning to look through his papers to see if I can find out." He hesitated. Moonlight reflected off the sand and I saw he was looking out at the ocean.

"When did you start doing that?" I asked.

"Doing what?"

"Looking out at the ocean for its opinion," I teased.

"You think you're the only one the ocean talks to?" he teased back.

Then he turned to Rick. "Uh, Rick, do you think you could do the same at your Dad's place? The investigation would speed up if I knew what was going to happen to Billy B.'s half of the business."

"Whoa," I said. "Is that cricket?" Here I stopped to look at Lady Anthea. She didn't move a muscle. "Do they still use that term?"

Lady Anthea shook her head. "Haven't in an age."

"That's a shame," I said. "Anyway, you're asking him to get you incriminating evidence on his own father."

"Ah, that's okay," Rick said, "but I can't do it. Wouldn't be safe." Then he glanced at Dayle, like he really wished she didn't have to hear any of this.

Chief Turner's eyebrows lowered about a foot and when he spoke it was with gravity. "Does your father have weapons in his apartment?"

"No!" Rick said. "Nothing like that. It's just, well, as much as I'd like to just go in when he's not around, he has every kind of crazy security system he can find on the internet."

"So?" Lady Anthea asked. "If an alarm sounds, he'll be the one to respond." Since upper-class people don't point, she nodded at Chief Turner.

"He doesn't have *that* kind of security system." Rick let go of Dayle's hand so he could tell his story properly. "Once I went in to try to clean up and a canister of tear gas went off."

"Damn!" I said.

"I better plan on getting a search warrant," Chief Turner said. "Maybe I'll get lucky and find out what I need to know at Billy B.'s in the morning." He sighed and ran his hand over his head. "We still haven't located his next of kin. Rick, do you know his hometown?"

Dayle interrupted, "We didn't even know his real name until, until, uh, now."

We nodded, like it was time to join the others dancing on the beach. I wanted to change the subject since she had almost said "until Sue told us," after I'd been explicitly instructed not to tell anyone the victim's identity.

"I don't know where he lived before Lewes," Rick said. "Sorry."

"My next question is why did he pretend he didn't know the dog's name," I said.

"That has me stumped, too," Rick said. "He was trying to make a case to get the dog, and knowing his name would have been a point in his favor."

"It was like he didn't want *us* to know the dog's name. Does your father think Wags might be Billy B.'s beneficiary?" I asked.

They all turned to stare at me, mouths hanging open.

Finally, Rick spoke up, "That's the kind of thing *Pop* would do, so yeah, he might think Billy B. had left all his worldly goods to a dog."

"I'll see if I can get any information on the dog's background," I said. "I can do that tomorrow."

"Background?" Chief Turner said, with a raised eyebrow that meant he was laughing at me. "Like if he's been in trouble with the law?"

"Yes, that's something I'll check. The Office of Animal Welfare has records of problem dogs," I said. I didn't for a second think Wags had a rap sheet, but after Chief Turner's patronizing remark, I didn't want to tell him what I really planned to check on, since it was just an alley to explore. What reason could there be to keep a dog's identity secret? I wanted to know Wags's pedigree to see if money could be made with the little guy.

Chief Turner turned to Rick. "I need to finish interviewing your father. Would tomorrow afternoon give you enough time to hire an attorney?"

Rick nodded. "Fair."

"If you'll excuse us now, we have some dancing to do," I said.

I turned to go, but his hand on my elbow stopped me. "Are you sure you can't have dinner with me tomorrow night?" he whispered.

"I'm sure."

Dayle, Rick, and Lady Anthea passed us on their way out to the group on the beach.

"Are you coming?" I asked John.

He chuckled. "I'd better not. I'm waiting to have a look inside Martin Ziegler's car."

"Oh, about that car. It might smell like it has a dead body in it."

"Excuse me?" he said with, as some of my favorite books refer to, "more than a little heat."

"Easy now. I just meant that some of Rick's raw dog food is in it."

He laughed. "I better go," he said, staying. It was nice. "You know, I just realized what you and Rick Ziegler have in common."

"What's that?"

"You both exude leisure."

"I work very hard," I said in my defense. "So does Rick."

"I know and that's why it's such a mystery."

We stood there not speaking. Not needing to talk. After a few minutes he took a deep breath and said, "Now I am going. They don't have a permit and it wouldn't look good."

Chapter 15

Lady Anthea's Novice Trick Dog class had a maximum class size of ten dogs but had twelve students, since we'd included Wags and Howard Fourie's Ariadne. At ten o'clock sharp a pet parent stood by each dog, holding a leash in one hand and in the other the easy-to-open treat holders we'd provided. Joey accompanied Wags and Howard Fourie was with his dog, and he was sporting an ingratiating smile for Lady Anthea.

I waited at the back of the room in case Lady Anthea needed support, or say, in the unlikely event any of her pupils had an accident I could go for cleaning supplies.

She introduced herself for the benefit of anyone who hadn't met her during last year's visit or at the Pet Parent Appreciation Gala and then scanned the room. "Wow! This is—"

Wags interrupted her with a quick, medium-volume bark. It sounded playful, and we'd seen no evidence that he was a "yapper."

Ariadne did the same. Was she imitating Wags?

Lady Anthea ignored the dogs, not wanting to encourage talking in class and glanced back at me. For some reason her look was quizzical, which made me curious.

She cleared her throat. "The class will meet today, Thursday, and Friday. If you're waiting for me to speak like Maggie Smith and ask 'what is a weekend,' I'm afraid I'll have to disappoint." Everyone laughed. "We will not meet over the *weekend*." This time she did a spot-on impersonation of the *Downton Abbey* actress, and the pet parents laughed again. "You'll reinforce what your dog has learned. Then we will reconvene for Monday and Tuesday of next week."

Next she listed the tricks the dogs would learn during the five sessions. "We'll start with High Five, then move on to Jump, Kiss, and Shake Hands. We'll finish class each day at noon, but we request that you stay an additional half-hour. Recent studies have shown that a play session with the animal's favorite person, you," she said, moving her eyes to each person in the room, "helps your dog remember what he's learned. Sue will have a play area open for them. We ask that you walk your dog for ten minutes, then allow ten minutes of off-lead, or as you say off-leash, playtime, followed by another walk. Now let's begin."

The pet parents all nodded and smiled, but I knew her better than they did. I'd heard a bit of distraction in her voice; she was thinking about something other than dog tricks.

She approached the first dog in the first row, a Shih Tzu, and reached for the leash. "Who is this?" she asked the petite woman.

"This is Smoochie," she said, nervously, handing over the leash. "I'm Valerie Westlake."

Lady Anthea gave her a gracious smile, and led the tiny dog to the front of the room.

Oooohhh, I thought. That's Captain Westlake's wife. He'd described her as his "soon-to-be ex."

Lady Anthea was saying, "Since there are numerous ways to teach any trick, we'll begin with the most straightforward. Then if there's a problem, we'll add steps. Now, take two treats from your bags." She took treats out of the treat holder she wore on a belt around her waist. "Have your dog sit and reward him." Next she gave instructions on holding the other treat in front of the dog with fingers closed around it. Some of the dogs pawed at the closed hands and were rewarded. They were on their way to High Five-ing their pet parent.

As the lesson continued, I let my mind wander to how Wags had reacted to Captain Westlake. Thankfully, there had been no further cases of growling or snarling from the dog. Lady Anthea was trying to catch my eye.

"Wow," she said again. An unusual word choice for her, and she'd used it twice. "Good dogs."

Again, Wags and then Ariadne barked. Lady Anthea smiled.

She progressed from one trick to another, with some dogs catching on with the first attempt and others needing reinforcement. By the end of the two hours the dogs were getting tired and the pet parents were happy. I led four dogs and four people to the elevator and out to the play area. Shelby met us there and took over, while I went back upstairs for the next group. After another two trips everyone was outside, except Lady Anthea, Joey, and Wags. From the hallway I could see Mason was with them. When Joey saw me he waved frantically, and I joined them.

Mason pointed at Lady Anthea for her to say something important, or perhaps break some news to me gently.

"Wags and Ariadne speak German," she announced.

I stared waiting for more, but it didn't come. "Wags is a Pug and that's not a German breed. It's Chinese. Ariadne is an Airedale, a breed that originated in Yorkshire, England. Again, not German."

"No," Mason said. "They *speak* German."

"They don't speak!" I countered.

Lady Anthea raised her hand like a stop sign. "Do you know what an onomatopoeia is?"

"No, but if it's a German breed, I've never heard of it."

"It's a word that phonetically demonstrates what the word means. Words like ruff, or bow wow."

"That's what dogs say." I was still confused.

"It's what we say they say in *English!* Germans use *wau.*"

"You said wow and Ariadne and Wags barked!" I said, finally comprehending.

She gave an exaggerated nod, and Mason and Joey did the same.

"Okay, we know that Billy B. sang German operas at the deli. Maybe he heard German at home. But Ariadne lives in South Africa."

Lady Anthea shrugged her shoulders.

"Could it be that she was imitating Wags, since Wags barked first both times?" I asked.

"That could be," Lady Anthea agreed.

"I have to get downstairs," I said.

As they followed me out, Shelby made an announcement over the intercom.

"Ms. Patrick, you have a visitor at reception."

The four of us looked at each other and laughed. Shelby had sounded so formal. "Ms. Patrick? That's not a good sign." I turned to Lady Anthea. "All Buckingham employees have approval to go to any lengths necessary to take care of an unhappy pet parent and that goes double for Shelby."

"If she's not able to make it right, it must be bad," she answered.

"I'd better get down there. Our code is that if one of us sounds corporate the other comes running." I started to jog out of the training room but jerked to a stop, like a cartoon character, and turned around. "Wait, maybe it's just Chief Turner and he wants me to go to Billy B.'s house with him after all. But why?"

Everyone stared at me blankly.

"We all know the only time he ever calls me is when there's a…" I couldn't finish the sentence.

Lady Anthea clutched her pearl necklace. "Might this Billy B. have had another dog?"

"A dog can live without water for three days but would probably need medical attention after one," I said.

"If there's a dog at Billy B.'s house, the poor thing's been alone since early Monday morning!" Joey cried.

"Go!" Mason and Joey yelled, shooing us into the hallway.

The four of us took off for the waiting elevator. I was the first one to launch myself out when the doors opened, swiveling my head, searching the room for Chief Turner. Then I looked at Shelby for help. She pointed to Rick in our store. He was on his phone, pacing, and at each turn his ponytail swung around. I had never seen him more un-Rick-like.

Lady Anthea saw at the same time that the visitor wasn't Chief Turner bearing bad news, and the relief showed on her face. She looked back for Mason and Joey to let them know it was Rick waiting in the lobby. The two of them went to back up the nannies overseeing the dogs and pet parents in the play area while Lady Anthea and I went to calm Rick down.

The last of the pet parents stood waiting to go out the door to the play area on the side of the building opposite the store.

"Sue!" someone from that group called to me and I turned. It was Valerie Westlake, holding her Shih Tzu.

"I see Rick is on his phone. I don't want to interrupt so would you give him a message from me?" The words formed a question, but her tone said it hadn't been. "Please tell him his father's business plan with my soon-to-be ex-husband is not going to happen!" With each word she squeezed Smoochie tighter. If we were cartoon characters the dog's eyeballs would have popped out.

"Sure," I said, reaching to pet her dog and hint that a bit of gentleness might be appreciated. "Happy to." She turned and joined the others in the play area and I went to see Rick.

Dayle was there, too. She pulled our arms into a huddle. In Lady Anthea's first visit that would have earned a raised eyebrow, now nothing. "His father said he could look at what he's calling his *important documents and official papers* if you—Sue!—came too." She leaned back against the display of inflatable dogs I'd fake-straightened yesterday. Lady Anthea and I reached for her and each took an arm. "I'm okay," she lied. Rick's back was turned and Dayle kept an eye on him as she stood, obviously not wanting him to see that she wasn't feeling well. "I don't see how Rick's father could kill his friend, but it has to be him, right?" she babbled. "Billy B. was driving Martin's car. Martin got the car back. And Billy B. was left there dead."

Rick turned and his long, skinny legs got to us in a flash when he saw how pale Dayle's face had become.

He held the phone down by his leg. "I don't want this to upset you!" Then he lifted the phone again and spoke. "I'll ask Sue now."

I looked at Rick and held out my hands palms up in the universal sign for *what the hell?* "What about the booby traps?" I mouthed, "Why me?"

"I don't really know. I guess because you're a trusted person in the community," he said, sheepishly.

A voice in the phone yelled loud enough for us to hear without use of the speaker option, "That's not what I said!" Because I have hearing like a dog, I heard him fine, but since he was bellowing it came through loud and clear to the others. And he wasn't done. "She can come because I'm a leg man."

Chapter 16

Lady Anthea and I turned right onto Savannah Road, in the opposite direction from downtown and the ocean, crossed over Highway 1, and then turned onto Plantations Boulevard. Chief Turner had texted and requested the pleasure of our company at Billy B.'s residence. I had texted back asking if there was a dog there and was assured there was not. I'm not a vet but if there was a dog that needed medical attention I had wanted to be prepared. After about a half mile we took a left into the Plantations East subdivision.

I caught Lady Anthea checking her watch.

"Are you thinking about the class you have *sheduled* for two o'clock," I said, imitating the British pronunciation. "We'll be sure you're back in plenty of time for the agility class," I said to appease her.

"I'm sure everything will be fine. Shelby has all the equipment arranged," she said.

There was no need to remind her that it was her email with specifications down to the centimeter on where she wanted the bridge, tunnel, and everything else placed. That's how Shelby and Dana prepped for the class. Just like there was no need to tell her how much trouble we had before we figured out she meant centimeters and meters after those numbers in her dimensions. During our learning curve we had gone from thinking dogs in England must be able to leap over tall buildings to wondering why they needed a special class to learn to jump five inches.

"It would have been more convenient if Chief Turner had relayed whatever it is he has found in the victim's flat over the phone to you," she said. "It must be ghastly."

Ghastly? I never said my business partner was Mary Poppins. For her, the shortest distance between two points is a straight line, whereas sometimes I need sugarcoated detours.

"He did tell us what he *hadn't* found. We won't be walking in to find a dog who had died from thirst," I said.

We snaked around the townhouses and single-family homes until I saw the two Lewes police cars parked at the curb in front of smaller attached homes. A local locksmith's truck passed us on his way out. Chief Turner was standing outside, glaring at me and my Jeep. When I was close enough to make out the look on his face I could feel myself getting anxious. I saw more than his usual intensity. He looked vague and confused, and that worried me. For once I needed his certainty. Yes, even his rigidity.

I got out, closed the door, and stood there. I was thinking about how clear and even obvious Dayle had made the case against Martin sound, even though her conclusion wasn't what we wanted to hear. I thought about how much pain there would be to get through before the murder was solved.

Chief Turner walked toward me and stretched out his hands. "You okay?"

I took a breath. "There *had* to have been someone else at my house, other than Rick's father."

"The crime scene people didn't find evidence of that being the case," Chief Turner said.

Lady Anthea touched my arm. "Sue, consider that Shelby didn't hear another car. Not in the driveway. Not driving along the street."

Chief Turner looked at the door of the condo and then turned back to us. "You don't have to go in if you don't want to."

"You said there weren't any pets in there!" I yelled.

"There aren't! It's something else." He paused, then nodded, like he was agreeing with something, but nothing had been said. "Let's go." He turned and led the way up the short walkway to the front door. When he stepped onto the porch he reached into his jacket pocket for a glove and pulled it on before turning the doorknob.

We stepped into a small neat living room. Stairs leading upstairs lined the right-hand wall. The kitchen and dining area were straight ahead. A tall, muscular Lewes police officer stood in the opening to the kitchen. His latex-gloved hands held a camera at the ready.

The condo looked lived-in, specifically by an older man, and a fastidious homebody. There was a dark green plaid sofa and a simple coffee table. An upholstered rocking chair faced a television on a stand in the corner. There was a fireplace in the corner of the living room and next to the hearth sat a plaid L.L. Bean dog bed, with Wags monogrammed in red. What was wrong with me? "Seeing this is affecting me more than seeing Billy B. dead in my driveway. What kind of person am I?"

"I think when you saw Billy B. you had adrenaline spiking. Now, it's just, uh, it's just what it is," Chief Turner said.

I gave him a look, trying to silently thank him for saying that.

He cleared his throat. "Back here in this spare room is what I wanted you to see," he said, already headed through the kitchen. The officer stepped aside.

There was a small room off the dining room and John waited for me in there. The room was being used as an office and TV room. The desktop was scattered with computer paper. A step or two into the room and I was close enough to see that they were printed-out newspaper articles. Closer to the desk, and I saw one article included a picture of Buckingham's. Had Billy B. been obsessed with Lady Anthea? I looked back at her. She was in the room, but standing by the door.

Then I saw what was on every single article. "They each have a photo of me," I said, incredulous. A few pages had coverage of last year's Pet Parent Appreciation Gala. One was of the opening day. Another had the account of the arrest of the murderer of our employee. "I don't get it."

John nodded once in acknowledgement and then waited for me to say more.

"I mean, sometimes I even bore myself." I didn't know how to finish that thought and so I shrugged and threw my hands up.

"You're sure you only saw him at the deli? You never saw him hanging around the Pet Place?"

"Pet Palace," I corrected him for about the millionth time. "I'm sure. There are always people around me and someone would have noticed. Besides, I didn't get the feeling he was like that. You know, a stalker."

"You're too old to be stalked," Chief Turner said.

"I beg your pardon!" Lady Anthea said in defense of my, or actually our, years gracing this planet with our presence.

"The average stalking victim is eighteen to twenty-four years old," he said, without a hint of an apology. I let his comment drift off because something had caught my eye. I picked up one of the papers, then another. "Look," I said and held them out to John.

I pointed to the tiny script on the bottom of each page, with the printing details. "This wasn't some ongoing thing with him. He printed these the night before he died."

John took a page from me with the still-gloved hand. "And the night before he broke into the Pet Place." I let that go, too.

"I guess he was gathering information in preparation for that," Lady Anthea said, leaning over the table from the side.

John shook his head. He was inspecting the sheets of paper one by one. "I don't think he printed these out to help him case your business. The opening day photo is the only photo of the door. None of any windows." He stood up straighter and stretched his back. Then he motioned for the officer to come in and photograph the desktop. "Get each of these."

The room was small so I went to the kitchen to wait and Lady Anthea backed out with me.

Speaking to John through the doorway, I told him about Martin Ziegler wanting me to come when Rick went over his records from Mozart's founding. "Lady Anthea's next class is from two o'clock until four. We'll meet Rick over there after that."

"And then you'll work tonight?" he asked.

I cocked my head at the strange question, which had given me a confused, crowded feeling.

"You said you had to work tonight." Oh, he was talking about his dinner invitation.

"Yeah," I said, scanning the desk. I was too far away to read the papers and had already seen them, but it was something for my eyes to do. Chief Turner, however, had been leaning over the desk rereading them. Now he straightened. "This should be such an easy question. Who owns Mozart's if one partner dies?"

There was a table behind the desk with a computer and printer. Chief Turner glanced up and saw me looking at them. He called to the officer to take the computer to the station. I started thinking I should be more careful about what I looked at.

There was a bookcase on the near wall, and I went back in for a closer look. There were two photographs on the top shelf, one of Billy B. holding Wags and the other of Martin Ziegler and Billy B. in front of Mozart's, arms slung over shoulders and laughing. On a lower shelf sat a stack of opera CDs.

"Sue, isn't this where you ask yourself what would Elvis do?" Chief Turner asked.

"'Such An Easy Question' is the title of one of his songs," I said, turning to go. "But I have another question. Who killed the guy everybody in town loved?"

Chapter 17

Lady Anthea and I had stopped at Surf Bagel for sandwiches on the way back to Buckingham's from Plantations East. She, Shelby, and I were in the office eating and talking about Billy B.'s interesting news article collection.

"Mmm," Shelby said, rolling her eyes. "Their tuna fish is magic."

I held up my identical sandwich. "I'm addicted, too."

"For once I'm happy to have an American-size portion," Lady Anthea weighed in.

"Speaking of generous Americans," Shelby said. "Sue, did you mean to let Howard Fourie bring Ariadne to both the trick and the agility classes? Because she's enrolled in both."

"Generous? They're paying through the nose. I didn't have any time to talk to Howard Fourie—"

"You mean, grill him, don't you?" Shelby asked.

"About their desire to rob Lewes blind? That's exactly what I meant. Anyway, I'm happy to have another chance this afternoon." I turned to Lady Anthea. "Is it a problem for a dog to have two classes in a day, and for a week?"

"It's not ideal. Ariadne is young so it won't be too much physically for her, but it's a bit of a waste of money since she may not retain as much as she would if the classes were spaced out. We'll have to see."

"The father's suit cost at least two grand. I think he can spare the money," Shelby said, pointing at us with a pickle spear.

"How does Howard have time to bring her in for both sessions? Isn't he busy trying to rip off the town?" I asked.

"David Fourie is bringing her to the afternoon agility classes."

"Well, they love that dog and that should earn them points from us," Lady Anthea said.

"They want to go back to South Africa and dine out on the story of their dog being trained by Lady Anthea Fitzwalter for at least a year," Shelby said.

My business partner laughed. "Remember last time when I had to lay all that on so thick after we found Henry's body?"

"Yep," I said. "And we were grateful for it."

"We were so afraid no one would come to the Pet Parent Appreciation Gala," Lady Anthea said.

We finished up and went to the lobby to greet the afternoon students that were trickling in. At some point Chief Turner joined us. He was leaning on the counter to talk. "I dropped by to let you know we didn't find anything in his files. We *did* find an office safe. I'll have to do something official to get into that though."

"Like get a subpoena?" I asked.

"No, I don't need the safe to testify. I'll get a search warrant. Be sure to let me know if you find out anything at Martin Ziegler's apartment tonight."

He turned to leave but stopped when Shelby whispered, "There's Junior now."

We turned to see David Fourie entering the first set of doors with Ariadne.

"Wasn't he instructed to bring a standard six-foot lead?" Lady Anthea asked, her annoyance obvious. David had the dog on a retractable leash.

"He can use one of ours," I said.

David was closely followed by a young woman with long dark hair, dressed in skinny jeans and high heels. She was looking down and seemed in a hurry to come in. When he was between the two sets of doors he realized she was behind him. Being a gentleman, though maybe a gentleman and a thief of our town's property, he stepped aside to open the inside doors for her to enter first. She looked up into his face and gave him a smile. Of the two females, the young woman was the only one with any intention of entering Buckingham's. Ariadne had other ideas, as dogs have been known to do. She may have been tired from this morning's training and realizing she was being cheated out of an afternoon nap, she decided to rebel. First, she put her four legs in reverse. Then she lowered herself in an attempt to back out of her collar, bumping into the young woman, who stumbled. The height of her heels was not in her favor, but David quickly grabbed one of her arms to steady her. Since he still held Ariadne's leash with the other, he let go of the door they were about to enter.

As he supported her he looked into her quite pretty face, forgetting whatever he was about to say. Chief Turner, Lady Anthea, Shelby, and

I stood watching the scene play out between the two sets of doors. We supplied our own narration.

"Smooth," Chief Turner said.

"Steady on," added Lady Anthea.

The two laughed, a little embarrassed. David let go of her arm and held out his hand and introduced himself.

"I'm Julie," she said, shaking his hand, and laughing again. I was once again grateful for my dog-like hearing. I was also thankful she was wearing jeans because the cord of the retractable leash had wrapped around her legs.

"This is Ariadne, who's going crazy," he said, with a laugh, moving the handle of the leash around her back to extricate her. Then they turned to come in.

"She looks awfully sweet to—"

Bam. Bam. Their two heads clunked against the closed doors. Neither remembered David had let go of the door he'd been holding for her when she tripped on the dog. The "one–two" of their heads was, well, cute. The word that came into my head was *couple*. They could be a couple.

They looked at one another, laughed again and finally came in, ending the floor show. David followed her, staring at the long, thick hair hanging down her back. His lips were moving, but no bon mots, witty repartee, or even urbane small talk filled the lobby to impress her. Julie had seen Chief Turner and sped up to talk to him, leaving David and Ariadne in her wake.

"Hello," she said. Even her voice was lovely. Chief Turner gave her a nod but before he could return the greeting she went on, "I'm Julie Berger."

The air in the room froze. Once I was able, I stole a glance at Shelby. She had caught that last name, too. I ventured a look at John. His eyes had narrowed by such a tiny amount it would have taken some kind of nano-supercomputer to measure. Maybe something better had been invented. Or maybe we were all wrong and her having the same last name as Billy B. was a coincidence.

"I was just at my uncle's house and an officer there told me to go to the police station. I was so shocked by what he said that I didn't ask where that was," she said with a nervous laugh. "Then I saw the police car in the parking lot and thought, who better to ask."

John looked past her to his car. "Your uncle's name is?"

"William Berger."

I blinked. A freight train of pain was coming our way and I could do nothing but stand there and be there. I took a deep breath in and stood taller.

"Would you mind following me to the station? We can talk there," Chief Turner said.

"Has he been in an accident?" She looked like she was about to cry. "Or, or, is he ill?"

David Fourie was inching forward, the hand holding the leash stretched out. I looked at Lady Anthea and she took over.

"Mr. Fourie, please bring Ariadne out to the side play area. We're about to begin." It was a deft move to give the newcomer privacy.

He followed Lady Anthea's directions, looking over his shoulder at Julie, almost in a trance.

John looked at me. "Maybe we could use your office?"

"Let me clean it up," Shelby called, already darting back to clear potato chip bags and sandwich leftovers.

I welcomed a few more pet parents with their students to the class and directed them to the side play area.

Shelby was back. Chief Turner motioned for Julie to follow him behind the counter and Shelby and I backed up for them to walk in front of us.

"Shelby, is my son here?" Howard Fourie had come in and stood holding a brown six-foot leash. It was made of leather. Was everything they owned expensive?

"I'm here," David came in from the side door. Lady Anthea was behind him in the doorway, with Ariadne. "Thanks for bringing this," he said and took the leash. "I'd like to add someone to the guest list for dinner." There it was, he was again speaking like someone twice his age. He gave a slight nod in Julie's direction.

"Of course," Howard said, as he turned his head to follow his son's gaze. Julie was looking at the floor, but her beauty was still obvious.

"Ms. Berger," Chief Turner said, pointing to my office.

Howard leaned closer to his son. "I'll have to check with the restaurant." Then he was gone. Back to do whatever titans of industry do.

"Sue?" Chief Turner was calling me. I hoped he hadn't repeated it too many times while I was busy eavesdropping.

"What?"

He motioned for me to follow Julie.

"Oh," I said, when I finally understood he wanted me there when he broke the news to her. I did a quick scan of his face and saw no trace of condescension, or any sign he might be judging her to be some overwrought female, so I walked the few yards to my office.

"I need to see her identification," he whispered behind me.

I swung around and pointed my finger at him. "No!" I mouthed.

Julie stood facing the desk, her back to us. She turned when Chief Turner said, "Ms. Berger?"

He introduced himself and then me. Without euphemisms or phony familiarity, he told her that her uncle had been murdered. I was wondering how a man who looked to be in his seventies or even early eighties could have a niece her age, but it was a little late in the game to let Chief Turner in on my doubts.

"Would you like to sit down?" I was already guiding her to the sofa.

I sat next to her and told her about her uncle's popularity in town. She looked at me, turned her head to one side, and then she fainted.

Chapter 18

As soon as Lady Anthea had said goodbye to the last of her agility class attendees, we left in my Jeep to meet Rick at his father's apartment on Second Street, over the deli. Because we were charging so much for the classes she hadn't rushed anyone out. She'd stayed to answer questions and give extra help or praise.

David Fourie *did* rush out. Like he was shot out of a cannon, he was back in the lobby and scanning it to see if Julie was still there. She wasn't and he looked dejected. Shelby had helped her make a reservation at the Dogfish Inn, which was diagonally situated across Savannah Road from Mozart's. David wanted to invite her to the dinner at the Gate House, but I didn't feel comfortable giving out her cell number without her permission. I drove while Lady Anthea called to check on her and to extend the invitation.

When Shelby gave her the directions to the hotel, it seemed that she knew nothing about Lewes. Chances were she'd never been here before. After she fainted I hadn't wanted to ask her how close she and her uncle had been but I was certainly curious. Maybe they didn't see one another very often—but then there was the fainting when she heard the news that he was dead. Nor did we know where she had driven from. Would she feel well enough to attend a large dinner party? That would be her decision to make.

"How are you feeling, dear?" Lady Anthea began. She gave Julie the particulars, like the time and the location, and hung up.

"She's going to try to nap and then decide if she's up to going out this evening," Lady Anthea said. "I think that's very sensible. The girl is in bits."

I turned left onto West Third Street and then right onto Mulberry Street.

"Where are we going?" Lady Anthea asked, looking around. "Isn't Mozart's located at the next intersection?"

"Yes, but Rick doesn't want us to park in front or to go through the deli. He'll meet us on the corner and we'll use the back stairs."

"And I thought my family was complicated," she said, shaking her head.

"How is your brother?" I asked.

She hesitated and I wished I hadn't asked. Usually asking a friend about a family member is fine, sometimes even expected, but when the relative is a duke, maybe not.

It was the duke's poor business skills or maybe his inferior money management that made it necessary for Lady Anthea to give the classes at Buckingham's. Her regular share of the profits had kept a roof over her head, but Frithsden's roof needed repair.

Now Lady Anthea was fighting back tears.

I pretended to look extra hard for a parking spot, measuring the pros and cons of each vacant spot. There were numerous options since the season for the beach was months away.

The fact that the duke was still alive kept him from getting a Darwin award. As far as we knew from Google-stalking him, he had never reproduced, so at least he wasn't a detriment to the gentry gene pool. His antics did cause Lady Anthea great financial stress, which was high enough already from an estate as large and ancient as Frithsden.

Finally, she said, "He'll never change."

When I couldn't stall any longer I parked in front of St. Peter's Church. We got out and backtracked in the direction of Savannah Road.

Lady Anthea grabbed my arm and pulled me into Flowers By Mayumi. "Did you see her?"

"Who?"

"Julie Berger is out there."

I looked out the store's front window down to the end of the street. She was standing frozen as an English Setter stopped in a "set" on the sidewalk across from Mozart's. She was staring, head pointed toward the prey.

Chapter 19

When Dayle rapped on the window of the flower shop Lady Anthea and I were holed up in, we both jumped. That's how intently we had been watching Julie, and wondering about her fascination with the deli. Dayle motioned for us to follow her, but our bodies had to realize we weren't having heart attacks before we could follow even the most straightforward instructions. "Come on, come on," she was saying.

Lady Anthea pulled my arm and I followed her out. At the door I took a quick look up the street. Julie was gone.

"Rick is waiting for us behind Mozart's," Dayle said, already jaywalking across the street.

During the season there's so much traffic in Lewes that cars had to creep along, so we jaywalk. In the off-season there weren't many cars, so we jaywalk. It was only a problem on Savannah Road, where even marked crosswalks offered little protection. In true Lewes fashion, there were now holders attached to telephone poles, filled with yellow flags. Pedestrians took a flag and holding it up, crossed the street. Genius.

We found Rick and followed him up the back stairway to his father's apartment. He reached over to unlock the door.

"Wait!" I yelled. "What about a booby trap?"

"I checked for trip wires and didn't see any," Rick said. Sure, he sounded confident, but I noticed he tensed before pushing the door open, like he was bracing himself for the unpleasant job ahead. Nothing happened. No water fell on his head. No detonation of a sound grenade or anything else. He was visibly relieved and walked in. "He cleaned up," Rick said, sounding shocked.

Some of the apartments over the shops and restaurants were elegant, and spanned great swaths of the block. Martin's was not one of those. It consisted of a bedroom, plus a living room, dining area and kitchen combination. The rear looked out onto the canal and tall narrow windows lined the wall. The front of the apartment mirrored it, with the same number of windows. Two massive recliners faced a television.

I smiled. "Looks like he's happy here," I said, looking around at the tidy room. The furniture wasn't the latest style, but it didn't look old either, maybe it was just well-cared for. "Rick, what were you worried about? This is kind of nice."

"You haven't seen the bedroom yet," he answered.

I circled around a recliner on my way to the door to the other room, and the others stood behind me. "Is that what I think it is?" I asked after opening the door and walking into the room.

"Oh, my," Lady Anthea said. The room held a queen-size waterbed and more six-foot tables than I could easily count lined the other three walls. They were covered with mysterious equipment and appliances.

When we were all in the bedroom Dayle asked, "Rick, is that bed even legal? I mean on the second floor of a building this old?"

"Probably not," Rick said. Then he started laughing. He took off his baseball cap and wiped his eyes.

"What's so funny?" I asked.

"I just realized something. You're looking at the reason Billy B. stopped using Mozart's side room for functions."

Lady Anthea walked closer to the bed, keeping a wary eye on it. "Are you saying it could fall through?"

"I don't know," Rick said and dropped down onto it. He reached for Dayle's hand for her to join him. Unfortunately, just as he did, Lady Anthea was reaching down to touch the undulating mattress. The bed came up to meet her hand. When the bed's tide went back out, so to speak, her balance went with it and she lunged forward. Pearls, cashmere sweater, leather pumps, everything. Rick, Dayle, and I all dove for her but the bed was in such a state of agitation at that point that we didn't have a chance. It had the drop on us.

"Are you okay?" I called.

Rick apologized.

Lady Anthea was laughing. She was lying, or actually sloshing, on her front, which made it hard for us to get her on two legs.

Rick and Dayle bounded up and between them, righted her. Once she was standing she threw back her head and laughed some more.

Most people assumed Lady Anthea was several years older than me, but we're actually almost the same age, which is late-thirties and close enough to forty for a staring contest. When she laughed she didn't just look younger, she *was* younger.

Chapter 20

When we recovered from our hysterics we got down to the business of finding legal papers that would tell us what happened to the business if one partner died.

Lady Anthea looked at her watch. "I haven't had my afternoon tea."

"Can't have it here," Rick said, leading us out of the bedroom. "I'll show you why."

It was almost six o'clock, but because it was February the sun had begun to set. I stopped when I saw the view from the front windows, then the back. Fairy lights on the trees lining Second Street were lit on one side, and those suspended on trees along the canal glowed in the windows of the back.

"Now I see why he loves living here," Dayle said.

"Sometimes Pop is crazy; sometimes he's not," Rick answered. "Sue, this view is what he wanted you to see."

"Why?"

"He figured you'd appreciate it," Rick said with a smile.

I looked in one direction, then the other. "It's like magic. Anyone would."

"I don't know about that. Most people don't recognize the beauty of just enough," Rick said.

Lady Anthea looked at me, then at Rick. When we didn't elaborate she said, "You're certain I can't make myself a cup of tea before we begin?"

"Uh, yeah. About that." He walked over to the oven and opened it, pulling out two small cardboard boxes, which he put on the small breakfast table. Then he did the same with a shoe box from the microwave. "I know you use the stove top for boiling water for tea, but I've learned not to turn on anything electrical here." He turned and opened the dishwasher and got out a filled shopping bag.

"Point taken," Lady Anthea said.

We gathered around the table and each opened a box or bag. All were crammed with file folders, neatly labeled in an old-fashioned-looking font.

"This writing looks like artwork," I said.

"Your father is a calligrapher?" Lady Anthea asked, gingerly running a finger over the writing on the closest folder.

"No, Billy B. was."

"A true Renaissance man," she said with a sigh, as she read the folders in her box, one by one.

"That reminds me—" I started.

"She's no longer there," Lady Anthea added.

"Who?" Dayle and Rick said at the same time.

"Oh, you don't know about her," Lady Anthea said. "A young woman came to town claiming to be Billy B.'s niece."

"Claiming to be?" I asked, unhappy that that word was out there in the ether. I had taken the folders out of the shopping bag and was replacing them when I read labels like *Payroll 2014* and *Payroll 2015.* "She was very upset when Chief Turner told her Billy B. had been murdered." I turned to Rick and Dayle. "She even fainted!"

"Any actress can faint," Lady Anthea said. "She could be anyone. Did Chief Turner ask to see her identification papers?"

I shook my head no.

"I'm surprised at him. I recall him being much more professional," Lady Anthea said, with a tsk, tsk tone.

"I kind of wouldn't let him," I said awkwardly. "Anyway, when we were waiting for Dayle we saw her standing across the street." I pointed toward the Second Street side.

"What was she doing?" Dayle asked.

"Nothing. She was just looking at Mozart's," Lady Anthea answered.

"Maybe she was thinking about her uncle being here—I mean, downstairs in the deli?' Dayle asked.

"Or because she knows she's the new co-owner!" Rick said, holding up a file folder.

Chapter 21

We had left Martin's apartment, gone back to my house and changed clothes, only to head back to downtown Lewes, and end up a few blocks from Mozart's.

Even though it was off-season all the parking spots in front of the Gate House restaurant were taken. "Do you mind walking a little?" I asked Lady Anthea. We both wore heels but in the safety-first heel height. I wore brown velvet pants with a brown silk blouse with a bow, and three strands of my mother's pearls hanging in different lengths.

"Not at all," she said. She had changed from wool slacks to a wool skirt, but kept the cashmere sweater set she'd worn earlier.

We turned left onto Front Street and drove into the public parking lot at 1812 Memorial Park.

"The classes seem to be going great," I said as we got out of the car and starting walking to the restaurant.

She hmm'd in agreement. "That was nice of you to let Rick tell Chief Turner about finding the legal papers. If we'd learned his father was to inherit his partner's share, his innocence would be harder to prove, right?"

I nodded. I did want Rick to stay on Chief Turner's good side.

"I'm still on UK time, so I hope this won't be a late evening. You'll just do your snooping about the wine bottle glass chip and then we can go?"

"It's more than a piece of a broken wine bottle to us. It connects us to our past," I said. "I know I'm not explaining my feelings very well."

"Today when you and Rick were talking about people not wanting to have only what they need, I felt like you were referring to Frithsden. With sixteen bedrooms, it's more than we need—"

"How many bedrooms?" I stopped walking and my mouth hung open. That we hadn't seen on Google Earth.

"It connects us to our past, also," she said.

I nodded, managing to start moving again. "But, it seems like there's more to it than that," I said. "You feel responsible for it, right?"

"Yes! It may be lost, but not in my generation." She swished her hands together, like that topic was over and done. "Will there be anyone here that I know? Other than the Fouries?"

"I'm not sure," I said. "We haven't heard back from Julie so I don't know whether or not she'll be up to coming. I hope so."

"As do I! I'm concerned about the coincidence of her showing up at just this time. Is that what you meant?"

"No, actually I hope she comes because she and David Fourie made such a cute couple," I said.

Lady Anthea laughed. "Sue, you're getting sentimental. You do surprise me!"

A sign outside the Gate House said for everyone to enter through the screened-in porch. A line of three couples had formed, waiting to go in. I saw Chief Turner walking down the hill from the opposite direction, and I waved. He was dressed in black pants and a black sweater. I was surprised when he came up to us, nodding hello to the others in line.

Chief Turner fell in behind us. "Want some good news?" he asked.

"Always," I said.

"You can have your dog food back," he said.

"Just toss it. It's not sanitary so I can't use it. The good news I was hoping for was that you'd arrested someone for Billy B.'s murder."

He didn't answer, but then I didn't expect him to.

"What about Rick's raw dog food? Was it everything I promised?" I asked.

"And more," he said.

Once we were inside the porch, I saw the reason for the bottleneck of waiting guests. The Fouries made up a receiving line of two. Lewes is more of a *when can we start drinking* place. We progressed forward in baby steps, making eye contact with one another, sharing tolerant grins. Howard and David both wore dark suits and white shirts. Two servers waited with free booze on the other side of our hosts. One held a tray with glasses of Negroni. The other grissini, an elegant though hardly substantial appetizer. The stiff host handshake, times two, was followed by dismissal. An easily jumped turnstile at an Elvis concert was the most apt image of the way my fellow citizens acted when they realized they had regained their freedom and that expensive-to-someone-else alcohol awaited. I would be right there with them when my time came.

When I was close enough to smell the cocktails, I began eavesdropping in earnest. David Fourie's speech again sounded like the instructions to a board game, say Monopoly or Operation, peppered with pseudo-professional-sounding phrases. "We're one hundred percent now," he said to a boutique owner.

"Lady Anthea!" Howard said, with unnecessary volume. She submitted to his two-hand grasp and smiled graciously.

"Ariadne is doing splendidly in both classes," she said, as she moved forward to his son. To him she said, "She's a beautiful dog."

"Just delighted your visit to Lewes coincided with this evening," the young man said.

"Thanks for inviting us," was my pithy comment to the father, followed up with something clever about the relationship between our nice weather and their decision to use the porch to the son.

Lady Anthea snatched a glass and we went in to the Gate House dining room. I smiled as I remembered the last time she drank while jet lagged.

White linen tablecloths, black napkins, lit candles, and shining silver adorned the tables that lined the walls of the small room.

I spied the mayor and we went over to talk to her. "Very nice, isn't it?"

Betsy Rivard was our new mayor, but we'd been friends and her Miniature Poodle, Paris, and Scottie mix, Riley, had been regulars at Buckingham's since our opening. Lady Anthea had met her during her last visit.

"Oh, hi, Sue. Welcome back, Lady Anthea." She leaned in to air-kiss my cheek and then Anthea's. "Yes, they went all out."

"Did the city choose the Fouries for the commemoration event because they're from South Africa?" I asked.

Confusion showed on her face. "No, we had an open bidding process. Why do you ask?"

"Since the wine bottle from the shipwreck came from a South African winery I thought that might have had something to do with the decision to..." I let my voice trail off, hoping she would pick up. I'd already said more than I knew or even thought.

"Their bid came in like the others. Just a coincidence, I guess." She was looking around the room, in true politician style.

"Does the Groot Constantia Winery have any claim to our artifact?" I asked.

"They've never asked for it back. Just the opposite. This will be the second celebration since it was found in 2004. Back then we brought

someone from the Groot Constantia Estate here to celebrate the discovery."
She paused and looked around again. I stole a glance at Lady Anthea,
wondering if she was also picking up on Mayor Rivard's discomfort. The
room had filled with people. Betsy leaned forward and whispered. "David
Fourie asked to have it loaned to a museum in South Africa. He wants a
decision before they leave on Friday. The Mayor–City Council hearing
is tomorrow morning." Her eyes bored into mine. "Sue, be there for the
public comment part." She straightened and walked off.

"Can I get you a glass of wine?" John asked over my shoulder.

I looked around to see what else was on offer. "One of their specialty
drinks is a lemon ginger martini." He made a face at my choice, but turned
to go to the bar anyway.

"That's nice of him," Lady Anthea said.

"You champion him when it comes to me, but when it comes to his
case work, not so much," I observed.

She smiled and took a sip of her drink, but he was back too soon for
her to say any more. He handed me the cocktail and I smiled in thanks.
"It's been a long day."

The room was small and we three stood close to talk. "I'm starting
to wonder if David has as hard a time with his father's dog's name as
everyone else does," I said.

"It's not a difficult name," Lady Anthea said. "It's from *Ariadne auf Naxos*,
which is a serious opera within a comic opera." She drained her wineglass.

"I know less than nothing about opera," John said, laughing.

"I know that when Elvis was in the army in Germany he heard a song
written to the melody of 'O Sole Mio,' and liked it so much he recorded
'It's Now or Never' to the same tune. That's pretty much the beginning
and end of my knowledge of opera," I said.

"What's in this?" Lady Anthea asked, holding the empty glass in
an accusing way.

"It's a Negroni cocktail. It's gin, vermouth, and Campari," I answered.

"Oh, but there's something as interesting as opera you *do* know, Sue."
She may have said *Shoo*. "You know that Billy B.'s heirs will inherit half
ownership of Mozart's."

"Okaaay," I said. "Let's get some fresh air."

John's eyebrows shot up when she said this. "When were you
going to tell me?"

I ignored him and kept Lady Anthea motoring toward the door. She had
forgotten Rick was going to tell Chief Turner what we'd learned.

"It's bad enough you told me you had to work when I asked you to go with me to dinner, but you're withholding information from me. Again!"

"Julie!" David Fourie called out. Those of us in the vicinity felt the temperature in the room rise with all the warmth in his voice. At least that's the way it happened in my head.

As I turned to the doorway where David stood, someone standing by the bar caught my eye. Howard Fourie was scowling, his nostrils flared and his lips pressed into a tight line.

Julie Berger took David's hand and came in from the porch. She wore a simple, perfectly fitting black dress and heels.

Howard Fourie clinked his glass with a knife and we all looked his way. By then he had relaxed his face to neutral. He welcomed the crowd of twenty and asked us to be seated. Dinner was served.

Chapter 22

Only the real dinner would have to wait. The Gate House signature appetizers of truffle fries and fried brussels sprouts were on the tables, and waiters came around with napkin-wrapped bottles of white and red wine. Lady Anthea had recovered well enough without the help of bracing fresh air and we sat down. At the last moment she made a sprightly little shift to the chair opposite mine and voila, there was room for John to sit next to me. The choreographed move told me she was just fine. Mayor Rivard and Valerie Westlake sat at the next table.

Lady Anthea complimented Valerie on how well Smoochie was doing in the class. This was either because the dog was indeed mastering tricks after just one lesson, which was unlikely, or because she wanted to turn away and leave me no choice but to talk to John. My money was on the latter, and I obliged and turned to talk to him. It was the least I could do after the awesome job she did keeping her feelings about the name Smoochie out of her voice. From my vantage point I had seen her nose wrinkle, but only a little.

"Did you get Billy B.'s safe open?" I asked him.

"Yeah, the contents that seemed relevant to the investigation are in our evidence locker. I'll go back and look through it later tonight."

"Can I look at it with you?"

"Why? You already found out what we needed to know. Martin doesn't automatically inherit Billy B.'s share of the business."

I had my reasons for not wanting to answer him about what I would be looking for, so when Valerie spoke, I turned my head to join that conversation. "I don't know when I'll have an elegant meal out like this again. I'd better enjoy it now!" She spooned a few fries and brussels sprouts onto her plate.

"The divorce settlement talks aren't going well?" Mayor Rivard asked, helping herself to the hors d'oeuvres. "I thought everything was working out."

"I did, too. Sandy gave me this bull story about how he was going to be coming into a ton of money. Now he says that's not going to happen." Fair or not, it was hard to see her and not think of Wags's reaction to her husband. Then her angry tone reminded me of her message for Rick.

"Valerie, what did you mean today about Martin and Sandy's scheme?" I asked.

"They wanted to use Smoochie for breeding."

"Backyard breeding?" I asked. Lady Anthea's head jerked up and I looked across to her. "You must think the same as I do on that topic."

"I'm extremely opposed to it. It's highly irresponsible," Lady Anthea said.

Valerie was nodding furiously. "Sue, I read your newsletter article about it so I knew how you felt."

"Was that his plan?" Betsy asked. "Doesn't sound like much money in *that*."

"No, it was something else, but he wouldn't tell me what it was."

"Did he tell you about our Monday morning trip to the Harbor of Refuuuu? Ow." John had stepped on my toes under the table, but when I looked at him his face was sweet as a puppy's. "You're off duty. I'm not," I whispered. I turned back to get Valerie's answer. "Ow!" That toe-trodding had come from in front of me. If there had been the slightest doubt who the trodder was, the look on Lady Anthea's face told me she was the guilty party.

"Betsy, I'm anxious to see some of the artifacts recovered from the *Severn*," Lady Anthea said.

I had taken a sip of wine and spit it across the table. Later, when we were doing our serious sitting and talking, we'd definitely be discussing this sudden uptick of interest. John was leaning over with a napkin blotting at the tablecloth. Then he dabbed my chin. I took the opportunity to whisper to him, "You and she refer to the main piece of our collection as just the bottom of a broken wine bottle. Both of you laughed at us. Now she's anxious to see our *artifacts*?" I drew out the last word the way they did.

My phone rang and I reached for it and stood. "I'm going outside to answer this—if I can still walk." I could see from the screen that this was a call I wanted to take.

I had made time during the afternoon to learn what I could about Wags. Martin Ziegler wanted him and I was curious to find out why. Now a friend who worked at the American Kennel Club and was also a freelance writer was calling me back. Hopefully he'd had more success than I had. I sat at a table on the porch. The temperature had turned chilly but the winter ocean air was delicious.

Kyle O'Malley was his usual New Yorker hipster self trying to conceal enthusiasm for anything. "Sue." It was a statement.

"Kyle." Then I laughed.

"Promise I can write a story about this. Only me."

"There's something to write about?" I couldn't even try the droll, no-enthusiasm thing after the hope I felt starting. I heard the tinkle of cutlery on a wine stem from inside the restaurant. Then Howard Fourie made a lame joke about his South African accent.

"He won at Westminster Kennel Club Dog Show," Kyle said.

Now Fourie was introducing Mayor Rivard.

"You mean Best of Breed?" I asked.

"I mean Best in Show. He was *America's Dog.*"

I heard laughter, the polite kind meant for dinner parties, not the real something was funny kind, and could make out the mayor's feminine laugh contrasting with Howard Fourie's full-throated guffaw.

"Sure, you can write about him."

"Not so much about the dog," Kyle said. "I'm interested in his previous owner."

Valerie's voice drifted out, but not loud enough for me to make out any words. Then I thought about what she'd said. I imagined model train cars clicking together. Captain Sandy Westlake and Martin Ziegler had planned to use Wags for breeding. After all, if Westlake wanted to breed Smoochie, why not try to breed Wags also? Then another click. I thought about Wags's fearful reaction to the man. Captain Sandy had taken Wags to the lighthouse and left him there. Did this mean the timing of the trip out to the Harbor of Refuge Lighthouse to get him *was* a coincidence? It had been all about the dog? Chief Turner and I hadn't been lured away from Lewes. The dog abandoned on the lighthouse had nothing to do with Billy B.'s murder. But I hadn't been the only one speculating that the dog abandoned on the Harbor of Refuge Lighthouse had something to do with the murder. Hadn't Chief Turner said, over and over, something about law enforcement professionals not believing in coincidences? The boat pilot had seen the dog and alerted the authorities and that was all I knew for sure.

"Sue?" This time it *was* a question.

"Sorry. She was an opera singer, right?"

"She was one of the most famous German opera singers of the last century," Kyle said.

Something was in front of me and I couldn't see. I almost screamed but I caught myself when I realized it was John wrapping his sweater around my shoulders.

"Are you all right?" he asked.

I nodded. Then I thanked Kyle and told him goodnight. I looked up at John. "Let's talk."

He pulled the chair next to mine closer and sat. In the background, Howard Fourie was introducing his son with humble bragging. It had something to do with UNESCO and I figured Lady Anthea could fill me in later.

I told John what I'd learned about Wags's illustrious backstory. He leaned back and stretched his long legs. Then he just looked at me.

"Well? Aren't you surprised?" I asked.

"At what? I don't get why anyone would want a dog, much less steal to get one."

I rolled my eyes and blew out a puff of air in exasperation. "Wags is famous. And he's living in Lewes under an assumed name."

John moaned and ran his hand over his short hair. "What?"

"How many people, other than Lady Anthea, would think of Wagner, when they heard Wags?" I asked.

"You realize you're saying that Billy B. gave his dog an alias that hid his identity as *America's Dog.*"

"Who else? It's not like the Pug went around town saying, 'Call me Wags.'" I started laughing.

"Maybe he had business cards printed up," John said. Then we were both laughing. "This only interests me because it might be a motive for Martin Ziegler to kill his business partner. And that's highly unlikely. What *is* likely is that Martin killed Billy B. either in anger over the theft of the car or to get his share of the business."

I heard oohs and ahs coming from the dining room and saw flashes of members of the wait staff going from the kitchen to the tables, so I stood up. "I guess we'd better go back in."

John stood but hesitated, rather than following me. Once inside I turned back to see him approaching Julie and David's table. He positioned himself so I couldn't hear what he was saying.

"Allow me. I'll order a drink." Lady Anthea whispered. My wingman chose that moment to go to the bar where she could eavesdrop more productively.

"Where are you sitting? We'll bring the wine to you," the bartender said. Would she be thwarted in her mission?

"I just wanted to compliment you all on the, the, those drinks you served on the porch," she said and returned. No, she would not be.

John was on his way over to us and Lady Anthea spoke quickly. "He wants to interview Julie Berger in the morning. She doesn't know if she'll be up to it. Junior says…."

"Want me to take the story from here, Lady Anthea?" Chief Turner said.

Her nod said, "Be my guest."

"David Fourie says she shouldn't do anything that will upset her further."

All three of us rolled our eyes. We stopped speaking when the waiter delivered plates with salmon and grilled vegetables.

Lady Anthea spoke first. "Do you think that fainting spell was put on?"

I shrugged. "Looked real to me, but what do I know? Maybe she's just that fragile." I held my wineglass up to John. "You can say I told you so, if you want to."

"Why would I do that?" he asked.

"Because there weren't any photos of her in Billy B.'s condo. Not a single one," I said.

To avoid looking him in the eye, in case he was gloating, I scanned the room. David had switched sides of the table from his chair to the bench. Now he was sitting next to Julie instead of across from her. He reached his arm over the seat back, so it was around her shoulders. Then he leaned closer. Now he was facing us and I could hear them better. I had to stop myself from thanking him.

With his right hand he got out his phone. "I'm not trying to big time you. What's your number?"

She laughed.

"Seriously, I'm gonna call your phone." I was struck again at how he *could* talk like a guy in his twenties.

Chapter 23

Shelby met us at my house after the Gate House gathering, and the three of us were sitting in the living room, staring at the fire in the fireplace.

"Did you eat, Shelby?" Lady Anthea asked.

"Yes, Jeffery surprised me at Buckingham's and took me to the Crooked Hammock."

"That was nice of him," I said. "Crooked Hammock is a brewpub," I told Lady Anthea.

"I doubt the food was as elegant as what you had, but we love the burgers and the beers. And yours was free," Shelby said.

"Oh, having to listen to Howard Fourie boast about his son felt like we were paying dearly for every bite," Lady Anthea said with a groan.

"I was outside, but I heard him say something about UNESCO. What was that about?" I asked.

"It seems David is currently vice president of the South African Commission for UNESCO and, if his father is to be believed, is in line to be the next president of the organization."

"Not head of all of UNESCO, right?" I asked.

"Oh, no, just the South African Commission, and at his age, that would be remarkable," Lady Anthea said.

I told Shelby what I had learned about Wags's title and what Valerie Westlake had said about Captain Sandy's plans to use Smoochie for breeding, and my suspicion that he wanted to do the same with Wags.

"Can Chief Turner arrest Sandy Westlake just on principle?" Shelby asked.

"We know he didn't kill Billy B.," Lady Anthea said.

"Yeah, I can alibi him," I said. "Unfortunately."

"Let's look at this from the beginning," Lady Anthea said.

"I guess the beginning would be Billy B. stealing the dog food from Buckingham's and from Raw-k & Roll," Shelby said.

"Who needs a lot of dog food?" I asked. Then I answered my own question. "Someone with puppies! Shelby, when you inventoried our supply, you said only puppy food had been taken."

"Or let's back up, wouldn't the beginning be when someone, I think it's Sandy Westlake, put Wags on the Harbor of Refuge Lighthouse?" Shelby asked. "Remember, the boat pilot had already phoned in what he had seen to the authorities when Billy B. was driving out of Buckingham's."

We did a little more serious fireplace staring, then Lady Anthea said, "Sue, you really don't believe Rick's father could have killed his partner?"

"That might be the only thing he's innocent of, but I don't think he's a murderer. This is what I want to know, if Martin Ziegler drove his car away, how did Billy B.'s killer get away, or even get here to kill him? The police have interviewed all the neighbors and the only suspicious car anyone saw was that thing Martin has."

Chapter 24

"Sue, look at this!" Dana peered over her computer screen and called to me from the reception desk. She had come in on her way to school on Thursday morning. Mason stood next to her, and bowed when he saw Lady Anthea with me. This elicited her usual laugh.

"It's six o'clock in the morning! I thought teenagers hated to get up early!" I had gone for my early run, showered, and picked up Lady Anthea.

"Other teenagers didn't get to solve a murder," she said.

I gave her shoulders a squeeze, wondering again what I'd started. "Your mother is going to kill *me*."

Lady Anthea and I joined them to see what was so interesting. The article from our local newspaper, the *Southern Delaware Daily*, that had mysteriously shown up in their online edition just hours after Henry Canon's body had been found was displayed on the computer screen. Dana moved the cursor to the photograph of Chief Turner and me. Then she zoomed to my face. That was the article that had threatened to torpedo our Pet Parent Appreciation Gala.

"Mason told me about a great facial recognition app," Dana said as she tapped away. Other photos of me popped up on the screen. She moved the cursor to show me the name of the app. "It's called HooRU." It was pronounced, "Who are you?"

"So this shows I'm me?" I asked. "Glad to hear it. Do I live in Lewes?"

"Yeah," Dana said, laughing, good naturedly.

"Even better."

"Let's try it on Lady Anthea," Mason said.

"Go ahead," she said. "I'm game."

"First, I'll take a quick pic," Mason said raising his phone. She smiled and he clicked. "Now I'll email it to Dana."

"And here it is," she said. Then she was tapping away again. "Uhh, how old are you anyway?"

"I beg your pardon?" Lady Anthea moved around the desk to look at the screen. She gasped and reached for her pearl necklace. "That's my mother." Her voice caught and she leaned closer to the laptop and smiled. "Everyone said we favored, but here the resemblance is uncanny."

"Yes, she's beautiful, too," I said. We all four had gathered closer to the computer. There was a photo of a painting, and it was part of an obituary or whatever the British expression for a death notice is. The woman's dark hair was worn in a conservative style and she had almond-shaped intelligent eyes, just like Lady Anthea. She wasn't smiling but she looked like she could any second—again, like my friend and Buckingham Pet Palace's co-owner.

"Could you use this program on the Fouries?" I asked.

"Whatever for?" Lady Anthea asked, pulling her eyes away from her mother's image.

"Lady Anthea, want me to email this photo of your mother to you?" Dana asked.

She smiled and nodded.

"Who knows, maybe they've put on events in other cities, or in other countries, and come away with their valuable artifacts?" I said.

"Valuable?" Lady Anthea raised her eyebrows.

"Okay, *valuable to the town* artifacts," I said.

"Sure!" Dana said. "I know they didn't have anything to do with Billy B. getting killed, but this is good practice."

I scrolled through emails on my phone, as Dana typed away. "Suspicious Minds" had been playing in my head during my run, and I hummed it while I emailed back to some friends. After a few minutes Dana said, "I need photos of the Fouries."

"They've been here for weeks, haven't they? There aren't any in the papers?" I asked.

"The father has been here longer, but David arrived the day I did, Tuesday," Lady Anthea said.

We heard the door open and turned to see Kate Carter coming in with Robber, her Collie mix. She was followed by Betsy Rivard with Paris and Riley. From the corner of my eye I saw Dana discreetly close her laptop.

When the dogs were where they needed to be, Paris with Joey in the grooming salon and Riley and Robber in the play room with a nanny, and the lobby was empty again, Dana said in a low voice, "That's just it. There aren't any photos of Mr. Fourie in the paper. Well, just his back."

"Still, they're in business so there should be many to choose from on the internet," Lady Anthea said.

Dana shook her head. "Their website has lots of graphics, but no photos of either of them."

"I didn't find much when I Googled them on Tuesday night," I said.

"Both of them will be at the city council's public hearing this morning," I said. "I guess we could try to take a quick photo then."

"Dana, while it's true that they don't have anything to do with the murder investigation, Howard Fourie is a powerful man," Lady Anthea said. "You don't want him as an enemy. We'll try get photos *if* you promise not to let anyone, outside of your mother and us, know that you're doing this."

Dana held out her hand for Lady Anthea to shake on the pact.

"Are you going with me to the hearing?" I asked Lady Anthea. She hadn't mentioned it before. "You don't have to since you don't have a dog in this fight."

"I'm happy to come to give you moral support," she said. "I'll be between the dog trick class and the agility class."

* * * *

Lewes has only one building for conducting the city's business, and that's where Lady Anthea and I headed as soon as the morning trick class was over. I saw on my car dashboard screen that I had a text. It was from Kyle O'Malley and at the next stop sign I read it. I saw he had located the opera singer who had been Wags's pet parent before Billy B. "She's still alive!" he had written. He was coming to Lewes that afternoon. He said he and his car were taking the Cape May–Lewes ferry so I wrote back that I would meet him at Irish Eyes. Where else should you go with someone named O'Malley?

Lady Anthea and I found a free parking spot at the end of the block and walked back up the sidewalk. She looked in shop windows now and then.

I pulled her elbow. "Look, there's Julie Berger and David Fourie."

They stood close to one another by the entrance to the city building. She shivered in the February air and he began rubbing her arms, looking over her shoulder with a dreamy look on his face.

"They've had sex," Lady Anthea and I said at the same time.

Howard Fourie approached from the other side and motioned for his son to go in. A balloon over David's head would have read, "Not so fast."

He reached for Julie's hand, in a *she's with me* way, and the three walked up the stairs and into the building.

"Hmm," Lady Anthea said.

"What do you make of that?" I wondered aloud.

"Julie's not good enough for the prince?"

I held the door open for her. "This won't take long. I'm just going to say possession is nine-tenths of the law."

We looked down the center aisle of the meeting room at Howard Fourie. He was talking to David and gesturing close to his face. I felt myself lean back from the tirade, even as I walked forward. For David's sake, I hoped he wasn't a spit-talker.

Mayor Rivard called the meeting to order, with a bang of the gavel. She read from her notes that the purpose was for council members to get citizen input before they deliberated on the loan or the transfer of the partial wine bottle artifact to South Africa.

"What?" I almost jumped up. "Or transfer? What the hell?" I whispered to Lady Anthea. "Even after what I'd heard David say on Tuesday, I held out hope they only wanted Lewes to lend it to them so they could show it in an exhibit or something."

"We have two speakers this morning," the mayor said.

Someone had slid into the seat beside me and I turned to see Chief Turner. He gave me a smile. He looked like he felt sympathy for me for some reason.

"What?" I asked.

"You'll do fine," he said.

I shrugged.

"Who would like to speak first?" Betsy Rivard asked.

Howard Fourie looked around at me, eyebrows raised. His voice said, "Would *you* like to begin?" But his tone said, "I want to go first."

"Please, go ahead," I said.

"My son, as hopefully the next president of the South African Commission for UNESCO, might be the better person to speak on this but he's graciously agreed to let the old man present our case." He paused, waiting for a polite chuckle. That South African accent caused a slight time delay in his humor. "First, Lewes does not own the article since the ship did not safely make it to shore to unload her cargo." He paused to let that *sink* in, similar to what the *Severn* had done in the bay. "I will not claim that the artifact belongs to South Africa, where it could have been used for education for families like mine for generation after generation. No! Cultural objects belong to all of humanity, past, present, and future," he said. So far, so good. He hadn't really said anything I could disagree with. "As world heritage, they are the birthright of all of us. These items, including the partial wine bottle, represent the collective human achievement of the transcendent." We were still talking about the bottom of a wine bottle, right? "To be used for education, artifacts need to be seen in context. This can only be done at the History Museum of South Africa. An institution that can preserve it better than a small museum in a small town." He paused and I thought he was through. Before I could stand, he was off again. "Fracturing cultural heritage by keeping the artifact in question away from similar pieces turns it into an instrument of division between two former friends."

Whoa! I gulped. Then I glanced back at the door. The room wasn't large, by any means. I could make it out of there in three seconds, four tops. Then I thought about how embarrassing that would be if any pet parent saw me.

I stood and took a deep breath. "He's not a citizen." Then I sat back down.

"That's all you've got?" John whispered behind me.

"You said this was for citizen input and he's from South Africa," I elaborated. The groan I heard from Lady Anthea I could have done without.

Then she rose. Good, she wanted to leave, too.

"Your honor, members of the city council, may I have a bit of the time Ms. Patrick has remaining?" She didn't wait for an answer. "Thank you. Ordinarily the transfer of artifacts is to right a wrong. There is no wrong here that needs righting. The transfer of the artifact would not rectify any injustice. The town of Lewes has the artifact from a good faith acquisition, and as such it is protected, even without proof of title. Mr. Fourie's claims are spurious and unsupported." Her accent took some of the sting out of what she had said, but I still would not have wanted to be on the receiving end. "Possession is nine-tenths of the law and it's up to South Africa to prove they own the artifact, something Mr. Fourie has not done. The wine was on a *British* ship, the *Severn*, when it sought shelter from a storm. Now for what Mr. Fourie said about who would be better guardians of the artifact, I find his comments offensive. Lewes has protected and preserved the item since it was discovered. There's no reason to think that will cease."

I looked around to see how this was going down with the city leaders. They were nodding in agreement. Lady Anthea wasn't done. "I completely agree with what my friend," she paused and sneer-smiled at Mr. Fourie, "said about the importance of cultural objects to all of humanity. Art connects us. Do you know what else connects us?" I almost said television. I was glad I hadn't when she continued. "Oceans," she practically whispered the word. "I crossed an ocean to come here. Twice. The town of Lewes welcomed me. And I will be forever grateful. I would suggest that the artifact in question has less to do with the history of wine in South Africa and more about the history of a town on an ocean. Thank you for letting me speak." Then she sat down.

I gave her arm a pat. "Thank *you*," I said.

The room was hushed until Betsy Rivard looked up and down the line of politicians and said, "Are we ready to debate?"

Several nodded that they were.

"Mayor Rivard?" Howard Fourie had jumped to his feet. "I plan to leave this evening so a quick decision would be most appreciated."

"Mr. Fourie, the celebration is tomorrow!" Betsy said. Was he threatening the city?

Had Lady Anthea overplayed her— no, our— hand? I leaned over to her. "I can't believe he doesn't want to stay to take credit for the events...." I trailed off when I caught sight of Julie, seated a few rows behind us. She looked confused, and like she was about to cry. She was staring at someone at the front of the room.

I swiveled my head to see who she was eyeing, like I didn't already know. David and she were looking at each other. She was begging for an explanation. He seemed to be saying it wasn't true. Then he mouthed. "It's okay. Please."

Then I realized Mayor Rivard was sputtering. "Well, well."

She had good reason to be alarmed. The Fouries' edutainment exhibition included an original animated film, with virtual reality characters mingling with the audience during the day simultaneously at several venues, and a light show on the ocean at night. Pulling it off required specialized knowledge and expertise.

I stood. "I'd like to make a suggestion. We could have a digital reproduction made of the artifact"—we were way past calling it a part of a wine bottle—"for education and research in South Africa. A 3-D version can be produced at the University of Delaware." Betsy looked at Howard Fourie, waiting for his response.

"It would probably take at least until Friday for it to be produced," I added.

Finally, he nodded. "That'd be fine."

The members of the city council began to breathe audible sighs of relief. David turned to look at Julie and I saw pure joy on his face. As we filed out of the meeting room, David passed me. He was hell bent for leather, or at least determined to get to Julie as fast as he could.

"That was a good idea you had," John said. "Sure saved the event for the mayor."

I was about to thank him for the compliment when he began mocking me. "Tell me, which Elvis song gave you that particular brainstorm?"

"Well, it wasn't 'Return to Sender,' I'll tell you that."

Howard Fourie came up behind our little entourage of three. "Lady Anthea, my side didn't carry the day, but I hope there are no hard feelings." *Cahry tha day.* I had to admit I did like his accent. He held out his hand to her.

"Certainly not," she said, returning his smile. He held her hand an extra beat. Were they flirting?

We went out into the nippy air and almost ran into Julie and David, standing on the porch. We were just in time to hear her say, "Take me with you."

Her voice was soft and they were standing close together. If they hadn't been standing so close to the door, we never would have heard her. The soft edges Lady Anthea's smile had given Howard Fourie wouldn't have hardened. Chief Turner's expression wouldn't have turned to granite. But, then, we wouldn't have seen the formation of a new, unholy alliance.

"Ms. Berger, I'll see you in my office within the hour," Chief Turner barked. "You are not to leave town until further notice." He strode away not looking back. He was headed to the police department entrance to the building.

Howard Fourie moved to stand next to this son. "David, you do know about the murder investigation, do you not?" Julie was standing right in front of him.

To keep from glaring at her, instead Howard's eyes tracked Chief Turner's broad back. "It's about time they made an arrest," he growled.

She looked frightened.

"Hold the telephone," I said. "Julie, he probably wants to ask you a few questions about your uncle. That's all." I looked at Howard Fourie. "And that's a long way from an arrest."

"Dear, I'm sure you want to help the police find your uncle's murderer," Lady Anthea said to Julie.

Instead of answering, Julie looked at her feet.

David answered for her. "They were very close and she's upset." He shot a look at the door Chief Turner had disappeared into.

"We're going to have to get back to Buckingham's," I said. "The agility class starts soon." We said our goodbyes and left the three of them standing where they were. No one was speaking.

"Oh, look at this!" Lady Anthea said, stopping at a window of a boutique of home goods on our walk back to the car. She was pointing at a dish towel with Lewes monogrammed on it. "Delightful!"

"Huh?"

"Get behind me and photograph David and Howard Fourie for Dana," she whispered. "Just lovely! So clever!" she exclaimed, louder.

"You're overacting," I said as I got my phone out. I snapped several quick photos. "Howard Fourie is mostly in profile. Let's go."

We walked to the Jeep as fast as we could, and I handed Lady Anthea my phone. "I'll drive by them. Try to take a straight-on photograph of dear papa."

I pulled out of the parking spot and drove along Third Avenue, as slowly as I dared. When we passed the group, Howard looked straight at us. Lady Anthea gave him the formulaic royal wave.

"I'm guessing when the queen does that, the other hand isn't taking photos under her arm," I observed.

"I should think not," Lady Anthea huffed.

"You were great in the hearing!" I said.

"As were you."

"I didn't expect it to take the turn it did." I turned left and then kept taking lefts until I was back on Savannah Road. "Why do you think Julie doesn't want to talk to the police?"

"I have no idea. David said she and her uncle were close, but it seems that would be a reason *to* speak with Chief Turner," she said. "I think it's odd she wouldn't want to aid the police."

"But were they close?" I asked.

"She knew where the deli was. That's in her favor," Lady Anthea said.

"Do you realize she hasn't once asked about his dog?"

My phone rang. It was Rick Ziegler and I answered it on my dashboard screen. "Hi, Rick!"

"Hi," he answered, not his usual casual self. "I'm at Mozart's. Pop says he can go to the police station now. Can you meet us there?"

"Did he get an attorney?" I asked.

"He said he's defending himself."

Lady Anthea buried her face in her hands. "Dear Lord."

"I'm right there with you, Lady A.," he said. I could hear the pessimism in his voice.

"Chief Turner is about to get a statement from someone else," I said. "Can he go later?"

"You don't mean someone else about Billy B.'s murder?" I heard that bit of hope in his voice. I wished I hadn't.

"It's his niece. Not really a suspect," I said.

I heard shuffling and then a door open and close. "Why isn't she a suspect? If there aren't any other relatives she'll inherit half the business."

"Rick, did you ever hear Billy B. mention a niece named Julie?"

"The one that was standing outside the deli? Nah," Rick answered.

"How about any other relations?" Lady Anthea asked.

"Um, not that I remember."

I debated telling him what I'd learned about Wags's celebrity status, but decided Rick had enough on his mind.

"You sound like you're in a tunnel. Do you have your hand over the phone?" I asked.

"No, I'm in the men's room," he said.

"Is there anyone in there with you?" I asked.

"Why do you want to know?" he said, starting to chuckle. "I'm not going to out anyone, so forget it."

"I just wanted to know if you have privacy. Can you talk?"

"Suuuuure. You just wanted me to describe some of my brothers."

Lady Anthea had been taking in our banter, looking at me and then at the screen.

"Seriously—"

"I miss this," he interrupted. "I miss sitting on our surfboards talking like this."

"Me, too. Don't worry. Summer will come again. It always does. And your dad won't be a suspect."

Chapter 25

When we got back to Buckingham's I texted the photos to Dana, then I texted John.

> *Martin Ziegler wants to come in*
> *and talk this afternoon.*

> > *Compared to who I'm talking to now, he's completely*
> > *normal. "Grieving" too much to answer questions.*

> *Tell David she can stay here at Buckingham's*
> *while he's in class with Ariadne.*

> > > *Why?*

A test.

Chapter 26

I joined Lady Anthea and Shelby at the reception desk. "Where is Wags?" I asked.

"Mason took him out for a walk," Shelby answered. "For the last hour he's been sleeping in your office with Abby. Lady Anthea, that trick class really tires him out."

"As it should. They're using their brains and bodies," she answered.

The doors opened and Chief Turner came in. "What's this all about?"

"It's time for a little less conversation," I said.

"Is that an Elvis song?" he asked.

"Of course. Did you find anything interesting in Billy B.'s safe?"

"Nothing we didn't already know. Nothing mentioning Julie," he said. "Stacks of old clippings that will take time to go through. I left them in the safe, instead of putting them in the evidence room. They're probably nothing."

"Was there a pet trust?" I asked.

He shook his head.

"Anything naming a caregiver for Wags?"

Again, he shook his head no.

"If you find either of those, I'd like to know if there's a provision for the care of Wags—the name of a caregiver, or any other instructions."

Mason, the reason for my questions on Wags's future, came in with the Pug, who was wearing another brand-new leash and collar, and I stopped talking.

"I need to borrow him," I said.

Mason leaned over and scooped him up. "For what?" he asked with suspicion. "We can't be too careful. He's a rock star."

"I need his help with an investigation," I answered, earning an eye roll from Chief Turner. "Would you leave before Julie and David get here?" I asked him.

"I'm going now," he said. He looked at Wags with such mistrust I was afraid he was going to Mirandize him.

"See you at three o'clock?" he asked.

"You will?"

"Martin Ziegler said you were going to sit in when he gives his statement."

"No one bothered to ask me, but sure. I'll be there."

With that he left.

"Mason, when Julie Berger comes in, put Wags down and let him walk around."

A few pet parents with students in the agility class came in and Lady Anthea escorted them to the side play yard. After a handful had reported in, she wrapped a cashmere scarf around her neck and stayed out with them. Though it was February, it was sweater weather.

The rest of us stayed in the lobby talking about what it meant that Wags was "America's Dog." It was, as Mason had put it, rock star status. Sometime around two o'clock, Julie and David pulled into the parking lot. He drove a rented Mercedes. I quickly threw a few training treats on the floor in front of the desk and went back to the other side.

"Put Wags down on the floor!" I hissed to Mason. Then I turned and called Abby from her bed in my office. "Come, girl." Since she's a Standard Schnauzer I had no guarantee she'd get up and come out. Being *my* dog and believing that commands are suggestions made her the canine equivalent of the preacher's son. This time she did obey, though.

"Hi, Julie," I said. "Good to see you. Hi, David. Hello there, Ariadne."

Wags and Abby sniffed around her feet and then in front of them, looking for the treats. Ariadne joined them, but David was holding her leash so tight, she was at a disadvantage.

"Oh," Julie said, backing up. She took David's arm. "I don't want to trip on them."

Both dogs snuffled and rooted until all the kibble was found and devoured. Abby went back to my office. Wags gazed up at each of us to see if anyone was in the mood to pet him.

I began chattering away, asking Julie if she needed help planning a service for her uncle. And was she comfortable where she was staying? I was killing time.

Wags had walked over to Mason to be picked up again.

Julie's eyes widened when I was in mid-ramble, but she didn't interrupt me. Finally I asked, "Is this your first trip to Lewes?"

"Oh, no."

I wanted more information, so I waited and watched.

"But I haven't been here for several years," she finally added in.

"Please let us know if anyone at Buckingham's can help at all," I said. It was time to put her out of her misery. I'd already found out what I wanted to know.

David put his hand on her back and they turned left to join the rest of the class in the side play area.

Mason walked around the counter, carrying Wags. "You wanted to know if Julie knew Wags, didn't you?" he asked, after a quick look around to be sure she was not near enough to hear.

"That was only part of it," I said.

Shelby leaned in. "If someone in your family won an Olympic gold medal, don't you think you would all be talking about it?"

"What sport?" Mason asked.

"Swimming," Shelby answered.

"Yeah, I guess word would get around the family," he admitted, after considering the question.

"She had no idea who Wags was!" Shelby said.

"More importantly," I added, "Wags didn't know *her*."

David intended Julie to go to the agility class with him and Ariadne. Julie wanted the same. Then there was Lady Anthea. Their fingers pulled apart. While I had complete confidence that they would one day gaze into each other's eyes again, and in this lifetime, they looked at one another until the door to the area set aside for the agility class cruelly took David away and my nudge to Julie's elbow in the direction of my office did the same for her. When we were in the office I motioned to the sofa. She smiled at the Elvis impersonator hound dog throw pillow, a point in her favor, and sat.

I wondered just how soon I could jump in to ask questions about her relationship with Billy B. Her faints and breakdowns came at very convenient times, but I didn't know her well, or at all, so I couldn't tell if they were genuine or not. I would start there. "We've never met before this trip and I'm sorry it's under such sad circumstances."

She looked down at her perfectly manicured hands, folded in her lap. "That's one of the reasons I've been so emotional. I didn't see him as often as I should have. I know that."

"How old was he?"

She looked at the ceiling, then back to me. "Almost eighty." It was obvious she was guessing, but that was close enough.

"And he was your uncle?"

"He was really my great-uncle," she said. Now that made sense, from an arithmetic aspect.

"Do you live very far away?" I wished I'd noticed if the compact car she was driving that first day was a rental or not. Could that have been Tuesday, only two days ago? I hadn't even noticed the license plates.

"I live in New York," she said. "I'm an actress. Well, I'm trying to be." She gave a little laugh. *Of course, just perfect.* I wanted to warn her not to tell Chief Turner about her career since it would be evidence to him and acting was exactly what he thought she was doing. Then there was the fact that in the mysteries I read young, beautiful actresses almost always ended up dead or indicted. *Not Playing Dead* came to mind.

"Billy B. was a fixture in this town," I said.

"Why do you call him that? Why does everyone?" she interrupted.

"That's what he wanted to be called. You know, Billy for William. What did you call him?" I asked.

"Uncle William. He and my grandfather were brothers."

"Were?"

"My grandfather died before I was born. Can you tell me more about Uncle William?"

I almost laughed but caught myself. That was so not how this conversation was going to roll out. "I didn't know him well. I think most of us thought we knew him better than we did. Turns out we'd known him long, but not well. Does he have other relatives? Chief Turner was having a hard time locating his next of kin before you came," I said.

"My parents died in a car crash about ten years ago, so I'm all that's left," she said.

"Was he ever married?"

She shook her head.

"Had this trip been planned a long time ago?" I asked.

"What trip?"

"Your visit to Lewes," I said, trying to keep the duh out of my voice.

"Oh, it wasn't planned at all."

"You just came on a whim?" I had been sitting on the corner of my desk, which had been getting hard, so I joined her on the sofa.

"No-o-o," she said. "We spoke on the phone every week."

Now, that was something Chief Turner could verify, I thought.

"The last time we talked, he didn't sound like himself."

Finally, we were getting someplace, but why couldn't she have told all this to Chief Turner? "How do you mean?"

"He sounded, uh, nervous," she said.

"Did he say what was making him nervous?"

She shook her head and peeked at her wristwatch.

"When was this?" I asked, sensing my time was about to run out.

"Saturday," she said, then she seemed to reconsider. "Maybe Friday." She stood and so I did, too. "That's why I drove out to check on him."

I didn't mention that she'd waited two or three days to look in on an elderly relative.

"I'm going outside to watch Ariadne train." She twirled on her high heels and was out the door. This dog, with the hard to pronounce name, she knew.

I followed her behind the counter. "Are you an opera buff, too?"

She froze. "Too?" She turned back around to me.

"Lady Anthea says that name, Ariadne, is from an opera," I said.

Her face told me she was filing that gem away for the not-too-distant future use. "And, of course, Billy B. sang opera to his customers at Mozart's." She raised an eyebrow and started to walk away again. I had another question, "Where was Billy B. from?"

"Our family is from Cologne, Germany."

I was about to go back to my office, happy that at least I had learned about her last phone conversation with Billy B. It sounded like he knew he might be in danger.

"Sue?" This time Julie's voice was stronger. She was addressing me instead of walking away from me.

I turned and saw her eyes were narrowed. "We're Jewish. That's why there are so few members of my family left. Neither my dad nor Uncle William would ever talk about it, though."

"I'm sorry," I said.

"I know," she said. "Everybody's always sorry."

She held my gaze for a beat, then nodded and went out the front door.

Chapter 27

"Here's my attorney now," Martin Ziegler was saying when I walked into the interrogation room.

I looked around wondering if his lawyer was anyone I knew. Rick, Chief Turner, Officer Statler, and Martin were the only people there. I was confused but sat in the one chair that was left empty. Martin looked at me expectantly. No one said a word.

It suddenly dawned on me.

"What?" I yelled. "I'm not your attorney. I'm not anybody's attorney. I'm not an *attorney*!"

John glared at Martin. "Mr. Ziegler, you said you were representing yourself."

"Same difference," he said, stretching out the words. Saaaame differeeeeence. "I decided to *choose* someone else to represent me. Tomato tomato." Toooomayyytoooo, tomahhhhtooo.

I shook my head, just as Rick was doing. I was starting to understand Martin's fabrications. They were like when Douglas Adams called the "Hitchhiker's Guide to the Galaxy" books a trilogy in five parts. It seemed he wasn't trying to mislead, rather he was trying to be inaccurate.

"Martin," I said, hoping he heard the threat in my voice. "You have hurt my friend enough. I'm going to ask you a few questions and I dare you to lie to me." No one was breathing in the room but me. "You see, I never lose my temper. I find it. And you have pushed me to that point." I was speaking slowly and clearly. I hadn't taken my eyes off Martin Ziegler. "You are in serious trouble. Billy B. either borrowed or stole your car and you got it back, leaving his murdered body there. Did you see him when you came for your car?"

"Nnno," he croaked. "He wasn't anywhere around."

"How did you know to come to my house to find your car?" I asked.

"I didn't, I mean at first. I went to Buckingham's and it wasn't there."

"Then how did you know to come to my house next? Do you know where I live?"

"I could kind of follow the car by the smoke and the smell. It's something I can do because of my bond with my car." It had nothing to do with his relationship with that environmental nightmare he called a car. You could have the worst head cold in the world and follow those exhaust fumes. I raised an eyebrow in warning.

"When did you realize your car was missing?" I asked. I wanted it all. Step by step.

Martin's eyes darted from side to side. "You're not much of a lawyer," he finally said.

I shook my head and wondered if I should leave, but I couldn't do that to Rick. If I did, I'd be letting Dayle down too. And Billy B. So instead, I gave him a laser stare guaranteed to make someone tell the truth. Right. Lady Anthea could probably do this better.

"I'm just sayin'," Martin added, having the gall to shake his head in disappointment of my work.

"Pop, no one here thinks you killed Billy B.—" Rick said.

He was interrupted by Chief Turner's throat clearing.

A chuckle escaped from Officer Statler, but she quickly regained her professionalism.

"Mr. Ziegler, this morning I reviewed footage from traffic cameras all the way down Savannah Road. They show you driving the car late Monday morning," Chief Turner said.

I leaned forward and said, "If my car was stolen, my best friend would not be the first person I accused. For you, it was. And you knew *where* he had taken the car. Had you *borrowed* something of his?" He looked to his right, out the window. I could see muscles of his neck tense and release, over and over. When he looked back around there were tears in his eyes. "Yeah, his dog. We were going to take good care of it, though. And we would have given it back."

It had not been my intention to embarrass him in front of his son. Murder wasn't the only sin that could make someone guilty and culpable. I would not allow Martin Ziegler to make me that person. He was just so infuriating.

"Pop!" Rick yelled. "Sue, don't worry about it. It's just something he does. He makes himself cry."

What had it been like for Rick having Martin as a father? How did he survive it? Now I *was* leaving. I stood and turned to Chief Turner. "He and Captain Sandy Westlake stole Wags and took him to the Harbor of Refuge Lighthouse. He couldn't hide him in his apartment since it's right over the deli. Billy B. stole puppy food to give them to try to get the dog back. Billy B. was trying to get away from someone that morning." Then I turned to Martin. "Be thankful that Wags was okay when we got to him." I was about to leave when the image of the newspaper articles about Buckingham's and me flashed in my head. "He came to me for help and I wasn't there. Because of the stunt you pulled, I was at the Harbor of Refuge Lighthouse." Was he looking for my help? Could I have done anything if I had been at home?

Martin shrugged his shoulders.

Then to the room or the universe, I said, "Until we know who Billy B. was afraid of, he's a suspect." I pointed to Martin Ziegler.

Chief Turner's eyes were on me as I made my way out, but he was talking to the recorder. "Sue Patrick is leaving the interrogation room."

Rick sighed and gave me a smile.

"Elvis has left the building," we said at the same time.

Chapter 28

Chief Turner rose, too. He nodded at Officer Statler and she got it, that she was being left in charge.

As soon as he closed the door behind us, he said, "Remember when I questioned Martin Tuesday night and he said Billy B. might have gone to Buckingham's or to your house looking for a dog to track Wags? You thought it was ridiculous, but maybe it was true since he admitted to stealing the dog just now."

"I still think it was one of Martin's fibs. There was nothing on the body or in the car with Wags's scent on it for a dog to know what he was supposed to be tracking."

He nodded. "Did you find out what you wanted to know from Julie Berger?"

"Yeah, Wags doesn't know her and she didn't know Wags," I said, keeping my voice low.

"So she and her uncle weren't close? If she's even his niece," he said. Here we went again. He'd labeled her a suspect.

"She said they talked every week and last week he sounded nervous."

Chief Turner was shaking his head and he ran a hand over it. "They didn't talk, they emailed."

"Was that Friday?" I asked, remembering how she'd corrected herself. Had she known phone calls could be verified?

"In their last email, he told her she was the sole beneficiary of his will. She doesn't come to see him for years, and then she shows up." He shrugged his shoulders and raised his hands, palms up, like, I rest my case.

I nodded. "So the timing of her first visit to Lewes is suspicious?"

"Everything about her is suspicious," he said.

* * * *

Irish Eyes was just up the street from Anglers. Kyle O'Malley was waiting for me at the bar when I arrived. He was dressed in black from his cashmere turtleneck and leather jacket down to his jeans and boots.

I had gone back to Buckingham's and came in with Wags in my arms.

He gave the dog pats on his back and shoulders. "Nice touch," he said and gave me an air-kiss. He had been referring to me bringing Wags for our visit with Pauline von der Osten, but the way he had patted the dog showed a nice touch, too. Many, maybe most, dogs hate to be patted on the head. They will tolerate it, but don't like it.

"What's good here?" Kyle asked.

"Oysters on the half shell," I said, looking around. "I don't think they're going to let me stay in here with him." We placed our order and told the bartender we were going to the back deck.

Kyle picked up his beer and followed Wags and me out. He took in the water view before sitting down. Being on the water meant we were colder, but neither of us complained. The Lewes Irish Eyes is on the canal and the Milton location is on the Broadkill River.

"Could *not* believe I found Pauline von der Osten. I didn't know if she was even still alive. She's in one of those continuing care places. She's in her nineties but she sounded good. Looks like I might be able to have a decent interview," he said. Then he got out his phone and took a few photos of Wags.

"Where does she live?" I asked. The waitress had brought a glass of chardonnay and I took a sip.

"Some old age home pessimistically named Autumn Acres," he said. "Sounds like spring's over, summer's done, you're going down."

"I don't think they call them old age homes anymore. I know where it is." Despite Kyle's dreary analysis of the name of the place, it looked pleasant enough from the outside.

The fresh oysters were lowered to our table. Wags got up to sniff but immediately laid back down. Not for him.

"Is it far?" he asked, slathering an oyster with horseradish.

"Nothing in Lewes is far," I said. I was thinking about the business's location on Plantations Boulevard. Billy B. would have walked by it every day. "I need to tell you more of the story. She gave him to a man in town named Billy B. and he was found murdered Monday morning."

"Fantastic!"

"Kyle!"

"I mean, not for him, obviously," he said. "Don't turn around but you have an admirer. Oh, he's leaving. Too bad."

I stopped myself before asking if he was wearing a police uniform, but I couldn't stop myself from grinning.

Wags had been dozing by my foot but jerked awake. He growled and wedged himself behind my legs. He wasn't snarling at anyone behind me, where my so-called secret admirer had been. Wags's reaction was to someone on the other end of the deck. I looked over Kyle's shoulder and saw Sandy Westlake. Suddenly Wags took off after him and when Westlake recovered from the shock, he leaned down and scooped Wags up. With the Pug under one arm like a football he turned to run. I leapt out of my chair and ran to the railing. I climbed over and took off after them. I decided I wouldn't be able to catch him since he had a head start, but I could embarrass him. "Captain Westlake!" I screamed. He had a lot more to lose doing this than the amount of money he would make from Wags.

He slowed and put the dog down on the ground. "Just playing with ya," he said. "Just a little joke."

"Right." I picked Wags up and walked around to the deck steps.

"Let's go," I said to Kyle.

"This is getting better and better." He paid our check and left a large tip. "Want to go in my car?" His car was a Porsche 911 Carrera, so that was really just a rhetorical question. I got Wags's harness out of my car. Once I had myself seated in Kyle's car I hooked the Pug to my seat belt. The engine purred as we drove away from Irish Eyes.

I was thinking about how annoyed I was with myself for not having Wags on a leash at the restaurant and what Mason would say if he knew, when the loud truck came up behind us. The gravel from the parking lot scattered. I looked at the side mirror and saw Captain Sandy Westlake. What was he thinking? "Get away from him," I said to Kyle. We zoomed up Anglers Road to Savannah Road, and turned right.

Unfortunately, we were still zooming once we were on Savannah Road and before I could warn Kyle about Lewes's low and serious speed limits, a police car pulled out from the parking lot on the side of a store, siren on. "You can't zoom on Savannah Road," I said.

"Is this what they mean by lower, slower Delaware?" he asked. Later, I would have to explain that those bumper stickers referred to the slower pace we preferred here in southern Delaware, but for now there was a police officer to hear out.

"Registration and license, please."

I pushed myself back into the seat and looked out the passenger-side window.

"Excuse me," Kyle said. He needed to open the glove compartment and my knees were in the way.

"Sue," Chief Turner said. The look he gave me was about as warm as what I'd seen on Abby's face when she saw someone was going away in the Jeep with me and it wasn't her.

When Wags, the little traitor, saw Chief Turner and heard his voice he wagged his tail so hard his whole body lurched on my lap.

"Sorry," I said to Kyle as Chief Turner ran his plates and license. "Hopefully it'll be a warning." Then I whispered to Wags that he wasn't supposed to be enraptured to see a police officer who was writing a ticket.

I was still looking out the side mirror tracking Sandy Westlake. He had turned right, as we had. Then he made a right onto Second Street. I had thought that was a good thing. Now that he was parking in front of Mozart's, I was rethinking it. He looked up the street at us and smirked. If he had been the one parked on the side of the road engaging with the local police, I would have done the same. Who am I kidding? I would have laughed my ass off. Then he traipsed into Mozart's.

Chief Turner was back. He handed Kyle his documents and said, "This is just a warning, Mr. O'Malley. Watch your speed." Then he looked at me, "Where were you coming from in such a hurry?" The question seemed odd. Why would he care? I heard a message in his voice, but needed a little more to go on.

"I think the name of the place was Irish Eyes," Kyle answered.

"Hmm, just got a complaint about a disturbance there. That's all. I'm sure you're in a hurry to get where you're going, but watch your speed." He had emphasized "get where you're going," and I took the hint.

I could either waste time defending my actions at Irish Eyes or I could make myself scarce before he got the details on whatever had happened there. I chose the latter. "Thanks," I said.

The powerful car floated up Savannah Road and crossed Highway 1. Then we made a left onto Plantations Boulevard. "Autumn Acres is on our left, past this light," I told Kyle. "Ms. von der Osten will be so happy to see Wags."

The two-story building was faced with white stone. The lobby was filled with sofas and rocking chairs. A fire roared in the fireplace directly ahead of us. A man was taping red paper hearts to the inside of a window. Kyle approached him and introduced us. When I saw who it was I tried to stop him, but I was too late.

"H-e-l-l-o, Sue," Dr. Walton said. Obviously he was still working off his community service hours.

Kyle looked at me, with a raised eyebrow, at the man's obvious animosity. I wanted to tell him that not every man in town hated me. Just the three he had encountered on this one afternoon.

"We're here to see Pauline von der Osten," Kyle said.

Dr. Walton pointed to an attractive lady wearing a silk blouse and jeans who had appeared at a reception window, and we walked over.

"Hi, Sue," Kate Carter said.

"Hi!" I hoped Kyle had noticed her friendly greeting. "Do you volunteer here?"

"Just a half-day a week. I wish I could do more. There are so many interesting people living here," she said.

Kyle asked her where we could find the opera singer.

"Oh, she's in her room. She's one of the most fascinating residents," Kate said, coming around and leading us down a carpeted hallway.

I noticed the poster advertising the commemoration events on an easel by the entrance door. "Wait, this date is last week."

"Howard Fourie came and gave a presentation to the residents since most can't get out to go to one of the venues," she said. "Mrs. von der Osten's daughter-in-law converted her old reel-to-reel tapes into a DVD and she's been watching it nonstop. She's enjoying it so much. She turned ninety last year and she has something new to enjoy. Isn't that wonderful?"

We agreed it was.

Her room had an elaborate Valentine's decoration on the door. Kate knocked and we waited.

"Come in," a heavily accented voice said.

"You have two guests," Kate said.

The petite woman was dwarfed by her Queen Anne chair, which was turned to face a side table, with a computer on it. All had been positioned to prevent glare caused by the sun shining in through the big window on one side of the room. She motioned for us to come and watch the grainy image with her. "This is the *very best* part," she said, with her German accent.

I left my handbag, which was really a beach bag, by her door and went to kneel beside her. She looked over and smiled.

"I'm Sue Patrick," I whispered to keep from interrupting the music.

Kyle introduced himself and reached over to shake her hand. Then she turned her attention back to the screen. "Thank you for seeing me, Mrs. von der Osten," he said.

"Please call me Pauline."

Two young boys were singing opera, in German. They wore matching short pants and what looked like dress shirts, tucked in. Their voices were angelic and they were freakishly talented. These prodigies did exist.

My bag barked and Wags jumped out. Pauline's hands flew to her mouth and she shrieked. "Is it? Could it be? *Mein liebling!*"

"It is!" I said.

Wags ran to her and I picked him up and placed him on the chair beside her.

"You didn't come on Sunday and I missed you!" she said.

I knew there was a chance Billy B. had taken Wags to visit her, but it hadn't occurred to me that she might not know that Billy B. was dead. From the corner of my eye I saw Kate tap the toe of her stiletto. I moved behind Pauline's chair. "Doesn't know," she mouthed. Then she shook her head and I took that to mean I wasn't to tell her.

I nodded.

"Wags and Billy B. visited her every Sunday morning," she said. "Isn't that nice?"

I would have to tell Mason and Joey about this arrangement, if they ended up keeping him.

"This is William, who you call Billy B.," Pauline said, pointing to one of the boys on the screen.

I stared, unable to speak.

"And that's his brother," she went on. "They didn't have to change their name after the war, but others did." She listened to more of the music before speaking again. "This was one of the most ruthless men in Cologne," she said, reaching for the screen, and pointed to a man in the background. He had been listening to the music with a scowl on his square face. He stood there in what looked like a gray uniform, along with jackboots. He was who and what the children were escaping from in their minds through the music they were making. "I understand his family changed their last name."

"What do the lyrics mean?" That was something in Lady Anthea's wheelhouse, not mine.

She dreamily rubbed Wags's back. "They are singing about families."

"Her daughter-in-law also put this on YouTube. We showed it in the community room last week so everyone could enjoy it," Kate said.

"And now both boys are dead," Pauline said. Even though one of those boys was in his late seventies, the pain in her voice was obvious.

If what Kate had told us was a ploy to get us off the subject of Billy B., it hadn't work. "I didn't know if you knew. I didn't want to upset you," she said.

"Most of my friends are dead, my dear," she said and looked at me. "The newspaper said he was murdered."

I nodded, then I told her about his body being found in my driveway. "I saw him and I don't think he suffered."

"Thank you for telling me that." She went back to stroking Wags's back, hypnotizing him. When she stopped again he nudged her arm with his nose for her to keep her hand going. "What will happen to him? We're not allowed to have pets here."

"That will be up to his great-niece, Julie. Have you ever met her?"

"No, I don't believe so, but William talked of her often," she said.

"I don't know if Julie can care for a dog. If not, there's someone keeping him now who has grown very attached to him. We'll see."

"Someone is taking *too* good care of him. He's getting fat."

Chapter 29

Lady Anthea stifled a yawn. "An early night is just what I needed."

She, Shelby, and I were eating Grottos pizza in my dining room. Kate had given Wags and me a ride back to my Jeep still parked at Irish Eyes and Kyle had stayed and interviewed Pauline. I'd made a large salad and we'd opened a bottle of Chianti that no one should be embarrassed to be seen drinking.

"Do you think Julie will want to take Wags back to New York with her?" Shelby asked. "If she does, Pauline will never see him again."

"I don't think Julie wants to go back to New York," Lady Anthea said. "She's smitten with David Fourie."

"Or she wants him to get her out of the country because she's a murderess," Shelby said.

"But if she flees, she won't get her share of Mozart's," I said.

Shelby nodded. "Either way, Wags is in limbo for now."

We ate in silence for a while and then my phone pinged.

"Here's a text from Rick," I said. "He says they're having a memorial service for Billy B. tomorrow at Mozart's at one o'clock. He hopes we'll be there. Want me to tell him we will?" I looked around the white wood table for their answers.

"It will be held at Mozart's? So, has Chief Turner arrested Martin Ziegler yet?" Lady Anthea asked.

"He's still letting Rick babysit him," I said.

"That's fair," Shelby said, reaching for a slice. "He's a business owner, so he's not going anywhere. Besides, any judge who's eaten at Mozart's would set bail at zero just to keep the place open."

"I never met the man. You two go to the memorial service and I'll stay at Buckingham's," Lady Anthea said.

"We can leave Mason or Joey in charge," I said.

She nodded and we went back to eating. I told them about my chat with Julie, and the inconsistencies I'd learned from John.

"So where was she on Monday morning?" Lady Anthea asked.

"I have no idea," I said. I helped myself to more salad. "I wonder if the reason she was standing staring at Mozart's yesterday afternoon was because she had just realized she would inherit half of it?"

"Could be," Shelby said.

"I remember the way she looked standing there," Lady Anthea said, "quite a tableau."

Next, I told them about Martin Ziegler claiming I was his attorney, and they howled laughing.

"What's that quotation, 'a man who is his own lawyer has a fool for a client'? Well, anyone who has me for their lawyer is a fool," I said.

"Do you think Julie and David will stay together?" Shelby said. "They met at Buckingham's and we were there. Maybe we'll be invited to the wedding. Wouldn't that be so romantic?"

"Stay together? They met yesterday! How can they even *be* together?" I choked on my pizza at how far Shelby thought their relationship could possibly have progressed.

"This is honestly like *Ariadne aux Naxos,*" Lady Anthea said, looking around at us expectantly. Why, I didn't know since we never understood any of those references.

"What does that even *mean*?" I said. "What's that opera about?"

"It means Ariadne at Naxos. Ariadne is a Crete princess in Greek mythology. Naxos is an island. You see, this wealthy—" she said stopping when she saw the looks on our faces. "Anyway, my point is it's a serious opera within a comic opera. Billy B.'s murder is the serious opera and Martin Ziegler is the clown."

"He really is," I agreed.

"Did he honestly pretend to cry?" Shelby asked.

I nodded. "Oh, yeah."

"Then we have David and Julie's love story in it," Lady Anthea continued.

I leaned back in my chair. "In it? It seems to me we have two parallel events. We have Mr. Edutainer and son trying to take a Lewes artifact out of the country. Then we have Billy B.'s murder. Julie is the bridge between the two. That's the way I see it."

My cell phone next to my plate rang. "Hi, Mason." I heard lots of noise in the background. Then I held it out for Shelby and Lady Anthea to say, "Hi."

"Lady Anthea, I'm bowing," he said.

"I trust that you are," she answered, laughing.

"Sue, Dana found something online that you should see. Joey and I have repeated what she did to be sure we came up with the same results, and we did. We thought it could wait until morning, but now we're not so sure. Can you meet us?"

I refilled my wineglass. "We were hoping for an early night. Are you sure it can't wait until morning?"

He lowered his voice to a whisper. "It's about the Fouries."

"Where are you?"

"We're at Fish On," he said.

"You're not too tired?" I whispered to Lady Anthea.

"I'm wide awake now."

"We'll walk over there," I said and hung up.

* * * *

Fish On was in Villages of Five Points, and ten minutes later we found Mason and Joey at the bar. Mason stood when he heard us and drained his wineglass.

The very shy Joey stood, too. "After we hung up, we decided that since Dana discovered this she should be the one to tell you. We called her and she's meeting us at Buckingham's." He was pulling on his quilted vest as he talked.

"Let's go," Mason said, already walking. "Put ours on her tab," he called over his shoulder, pointing at me.

"I don't have a tab, but I do have this," I said to the bartender. I slapped down a credit card. I'd brought it intending to buy the next round.

Shelby cleared her throat and I looked around. She was motioning toward the back of the restaurant. David and Howard Fourie were eating, and staring at their respective phones. Howard Fourie saw me and forced a wave.

"I wonder where Julie is?" Shelby whispered.

"Did you know they were here?" I asked Mason and Joey.

"Papa Bear walked by," Mason said.

"A couple of times," Joey added.

Lady Anthea began clearing her throat. She was nodding in the direction of the restaurant entrance. Martin Ziegler, and Rick, holding Dayle's hand, stood at the hostess desk.

I paid the check and we filed out.

"Where was Billy B.'s family from?" Mason asked.

"Cologne, Germany," I said. "Julie told us that today."

"Interesting," he said.

I figured there was more to that subject but we all wanted to talk to Rick, Dayle, and Martin. When the hostess came to seat them we said goodbye and started the chilly, but thankfully short, trek up Village Main Boulevard to Buckingham's at the intersection of that street and Savannah Road.

Dana was sitting in her car when we got there. She jumped out and bounded to the door. "Did you come up with the same results I did?" she asked Mason. "You did, didn't you?!"

I had telephoned our nighttime hostess and Taylor and Laurie were waiting downstairs to open the beautifully repaired doors for us.

"Is everything okay?" Taylor asked, her forehead furrowed.

"We need to have a meeting and this was the best time," I said. "I'll tell you all about it later."

They took the elevator back upstairs and the rest of us went to my office.

I sat behind my desk. Lady Anthea, Shelby, and Joey sat on the sofa. Dana's young bones sat on the floor, by Shelby's feet. She was carrying her laptop. Mason stood with his laptop under his arm.

"Lady Anthea, remember when we ran your photograph through the facial recognition app, HooRU?"

"Sure," she said. "You found the image of my mother."

Mason continued. "We ran Howard Fourie, and this is what the app came up with."

He and Dana opened their laptops for us to see. Shelby, Lady Anthea, and I stared. Our mouths dropped open at the sight of the man with a wide face, a big hand held against his uniform.

"A Nazi?" I croaked.

"This is Howard's father, David's grandfather," Dana said. "I Googled him. He was a big deal in the Gestapo in *Cologne,* Germany."

"I told you Ariadne was German!" Lady Anthea exclaimed. "Someone *has* been speaking German to that dog."

"They're not from South Africa?" I asked.

"This man and his wife emigrated in 1945. Howard and David were both born in South Africa," Mason said.

"But when he spoke at the mayor and city council meeting this morning he talked about his family living there generation after generation. Those were his words!" I said.

Mason said, "Cologne!"

Lady Anthea, Shelby, and I turned to him.

"Are you saying the Fouries have a connection to Billy B.?" I asked.

Mason, Joey, and Dana nodded once, unequivocally. Lady Anthea and Shelby shook their heads side to side. Once, and they were just as unambiguous in their opinion. We had a generation divide.

"Cologne is a big city. It could be a coincidence," I said. Why was everyone so down on coincidences? When did they get a bad name? I loved them. A book I'd read just last week, *The Porcelain Parrot*, had ended with one and it was masterful.

* * * *

Both Dana and Mason had offered to give us a ride back to my house, but Lady Anthea and I chose to walk. Now the cold air had us speed walking.

A Mercedes pulled up next to us and stopped. Howard rolled the window down. "Are you ladies out for an evening stroll?"

"Brisk!" Lady Anthea recovered first and said, "Brilliant."

"Aren't you cold?" the older man asked. The epitome of urbanity and polish.

I leaned over to see David behind the wheel. When his father asked us if we would like a ride home, they had plenty of room, would be happy to, no trouble at all, were we sure, I caught the younger man looking at the dashboard. At the clock? Wanting to be with Julie? We assured him we *wanted* to walk and I saw David's shoulders relax.

He offered again and we demurred again. Finally the big black car drove away.

"Do you think it's fair for Howard or David to be blamed for what someone in their family did before they were born?" I asked.

"I don't know but Howard must feel some guilt or he wouldn't have lied at the hearing," she said.

"Does he feel guilt or shame?" I asked. "I think they're different."

We walked on, thinking our thoughts. When we turned left onto West Batten we were ready to talk again. "I think Rick feels it, too," she said.

"This should make him see his father differently! There's really no comparison between a mass murderer and a clown or con man, or whatever Martin is." I opened the front door. "There's a chance that we have one opera now, isn't there?"

Chapter 30

The garage door purred as it lifted open. Abby was frantically barking. I was out of bed and running out of the bedroom.

Lady Anthea opened her door. "Sue, is that you? Are you—?"

"I'm over here," I called to her from across the living room. "Call 9-1-1." I remembered last year when she was under stress she had forgotten that we use 9-1-1, not 9-9-9.

Someone was trying to open the door from the garage to the mudroom. Abby growled and snarled at the door. She barked between growls. The volume was louder than I had ever heard from her.

"9-1-1," I repeated. "Then close the door to your room. Stay there!" I looked around for something to protect us with. I lunged for the kitchen countertop and grabbed my car keys, then I pressed the red alarm button on the fob and was rewarded with an instantaneous response. The car horn sounded over and over again, along with a piercing siren I'd never heard before. Never needed it. From under the door, I saw the car lights were flashing.

Lady Anthea hadn't stayed in her bedroom. She was by my side, with her phone to her ear. "I don't know this address!" she called out to me over the noise.

"They'll know it," I assured her. I saw her eyes were wide with fear. I wanted to remind her that 9-1-1 operators could tell the address of the caller.

She hesitated and then thanked him or her.

"Ask them to stay on the line with us," I said.

"Uh, she said she would. There's a patrol car in the area." She listened again to the dispatcher. "They'll be here—"

There was a crash of something hefty hitting the door, and I flinched. Lady Anthea cried out, and I took her arm and nudged her behind me. Abby sprang to the mudroom in one bound and her barking increased in volume, though I hadn't thought that was possible. She was sniffing the bottom of the door, then she stopped for a long, low, you'll-have-to-come-through-me growl again. Then her thunderous barking was back. Our would-be home invader was definitely still in the garage.

The door had held, but who knew for how long. Could it take another blow with the force of the first?

"We may need to go out the back door," I said, when I knew Lady Anthea could hear me.

Was that what we should do? We could run to a neighbor's house. Whoever was in the garage would chase us. Not could. Would. Though my mind was racing I knew that was our only option. If he got inside, we would run out the back door. "Get ready to run." I hoped my confusion didn't show. I needed Lady Anthea to run, but I also knew I wouldn't leave the house without Abby.

Between the blasts of the horn from the car alarm sounding, I heard movement in the garage. Then the car noises drowned whatever it was out. There was another crash against the door. Again, it held. The hinges, the lock, the frame everything rocked but stayed. I stared at it, as if the door might weaken if I took my eyes off of it.

"Sue, I hear a police car," Lady Anthea yelled.

I pressed the alarm button on the car key fob and the Jeep silenced and the lights turned off.

"Let's look out the front windows," Lady Anthea whispered. She was still holding the phone to her ear.

"Ma'am, do not open the door until instructed to by an officer," the dispatcher said.

I looked at Abby for a true read of the situation, knowing I could rely on her. She had relaxed, though only slightly, and was looking up at me with her glossy brown eyes. I looked through the kitchen to the dining room window and saw a flashing red light. Then I turned back to the garage door. Nothing from there. We went to the living room and waited. Lady Anthea collapsed onto the sofa and I propped myself on the arm of a chair by the door. The patrol car lights strobed through the room and I, for one, let myself be mesmerized. I leaned over and rubbed Abby's back. "Good girl."

I jumped at the knock on the door.

"Sue," John called.

I opened the door. "Are you always on duty—"

He grabbed me in his arms and pulled me in so tight my face was smushed and contorted into his uniform. I smelled soap and cold night air. I heard him breathing. Then he pulled one arm back and held it up in a stop sign to whoever was behind him. He took a deep breath in, exhaled, then let me go. At first I stumbled from being lowered down by an inch or so. "Sorry," he said, but not to me. He was talking to Officer Statler. "Just needed a second."

They came in and he looked to me. Lady Anthea had turned on a lamp at some point.

"So, you haven't changed your garage door code," John said.

Chapter 31

Lady Anthea had insisted on making tea and we sat at the dining room table. John, who was back to being Chief Turner, was not a fan and hadn't touched his mug. He stared at his little black notebook, and Officer Statler, with a computer tablet, was typing away. We had seen what the intruder had done to the garage side of my poor door. No one had a guess at what he'd hit it with, but it had been heavy and the blows had been powerful.

"If you want to file a claim against your homeowner's insurance policy for replacement of that door, stop by the station and we'll give you the documentation you need," he said.

I shook my head. "That door is like my best friend right now."

"Mine, too," Lady Anthea said. She had put a robe over her nightgown, but kept pressing her hands against her hair. She was obviously unaccustomed to being seen in such an intimate state. I was wearing flannel pajamas and socks. "Seeing the other side, I can't believe he didn't knock it in."

"I think it was a *he,* too," Chief Turner said. "I only saw an outline when I chased him down the street, but..." He let the sentence go when he went back to writing in his notebook.

In the background Officer Statler typed away on the keyboard screen. "Neither of you heard him speak?" she asked us.

Lady Anthea and I shook our heads.

"So we have no idea who it was," Chief Turner said, closing the notebook, and Officer Statler closed the tablet. "Damn."

"It was Billy B.'s killer," I said.

Chief Turner looked at me and raised his eyebrow. A hint of a grin was the tipoff that I was right, or at least onto something. "You know that how?"

"He saw the garage door code Billy B. used. Only Billy B. didn't get all the numbers entered. He would have seen it when he was behind him about to hit him over the head. And it was someone who doesn't know me." I added the last part just to show off.

"Now you've lost me," Lady Anthea said.

"Those blows showed a lot of anger. If you really wanted to hurt me, and knew me, what would you do?" I asked.

Chief Turner smiled and answered, "You'd whack that Jeep, at least on your way out."

Lady Anthea exclaimed, "And, why not? Obviously, he had something to do that with right in his hand." She showed us her palm, as if that proved her point.

John stood. "I want to look at the garage again just to be sure the weapon wasn't something he picked up in there."

Officer Statler stood to go with him. "Lady Anthea, would you go over your recollections again, just to be sure we have it all?" The officer sat back down and looked at Anthea. "Sue?" Chief Turner said.

I took that as a hint that I was supposed to go with him and so I led him through the kitchen.

When we got to the garage he looked at the collection of pooper scoopers, garden tools and brooms hanging on the wall.

"Nothing looks bent," I said.

He turned and looked down at me. "Uh, that guy today?" At first I thought he meant the person who had tried to break in. Then he added, "Was he anybody?" Oh, he meant Kyle.

I shook my head no. "I hope he's somebody to someone, but to me, he's a friend."

"I'm sorry about, well, that." He pointed toward the inside of the house.

"You mean for grabbing me? Like this?" Of course, *his* feet stayed on the ground when I lunged and caught him in a bear hug.

Chapter 32

On my Friday morning run, once again I had Elvis's song, "Suspicious Minds," in my head. I figured it must be there for a reason. I just didn't know what it was yet. Maybe my brain needed something to think about other than last night's near break-in. I had been terrified. I had tried to act as if it was nothing, and now I felt like if I made one wrong move I would be exposed for the fraud I was. And I knew I would go through the day pretending and hoping John Turner would only see me "exuding leisure," the way he'd described me on Tuesday night. The Lewes police hadn't caught him. Yet. Whoever he was, he had used gloves when he entered that ill-advised, *former,* code on the keypad for the garage door opener. And now I was having a hard time getting in enough air.

When I got back home, Lady Anthea was up and having breakfast.

"I thought you'd be having a *lie-in,*" I said, still playacting, joking and using one of her British-isms as an easy prop for my disguise.

"I couldn't get back to sleep," she said, pouring hot water over a tea bag, and gazing down on it as if mentally saying, "Look what's become of me."

"If you want to go back to bed, I can wake you in time for the trick class," I offered.

She shook her head. "What are we going to do?"

I started to say lock the doors but she wasn't done. "The Fouries are leaving tonight and Julie Berger could be going with them."

She wasn't talking about last night; she was referring to Billy B.'s murder. That change of subject reassured me of her emotional state and I smiled.

"Julie won't be going with them if the father has anything to do with it," I said. "For some reason he disapproves of her."

"My father was like that about several of my boyfriends."

"But not the man you eventually married?" I asked.

"Oh, my, no. He was a catch."

"I wish I could have met him," I said. "I bet he would be proud of all you've done in the last few years."

"If he was still alive I wouldn't have moved back to my family home, Frithsden." She put her teacup in the dishwasher, humming a bit. "I have a tune in my head," she said.

"Me, too! Wouldn't it be something if it was the same song!" We would be like those sorority girls whose periods come at the same time each month when they live together. "You go first. What's yours?"

"Mine is quite well known, and we've been thinking a lot this week about German operas." I wanted to stop her there to correct the *we* part, but between Billy B. and Pauline, she was right. "The songs in our heads could be the same." She was smiling. I think she had even forgiven her tea for being the bag kind. "It's the prelude to act one of Wagner's *Lohengrin*. 'The Wedding Chorus' is in act three, though you probably know it as 'Here Comes the Bride.' Hold on there. Was that the music you were hearing, too?"

"Not exactly," I said. "I feel like mine is trying to tell me something. Do you think your song means anything?"

"Suuueee, tell me your song."

I told her it was "Suspicious Minds" and she shook her head. "Are you saying Elvis was psychic?"

"No, I'm not saying that."

"Then how could he have presaged last night's attack?" Presaged is the kind of word Lady Anthea threw at me from time to time. "Or are you saying he knew we would be stuck solving this case?"

"We are stuck! I have no idea who killed Billy B." I grabbed a banana. "What was that opera about? Let's see if Wagner, the composer, not the dog, helps us out any more."

"In *Lohengrin*, a knight in shining armor asks the heroine if he can be her protector, and he asks her to marry him, but tells her she must never ask him his name or where he came from. She promises never to pose the forbidden question," Lady Anthea explained with a dreamy look in her eyes.

"I always thought Chief Turner was secretive about his life before Lewes, but your guy beats him. She can't even ask?" I rolled my eyes. "That is a perfect example to show why I'm not interested in getting married. But look on the bright side, she'll be keeping her maiden name. Good for her."

"Don't you see? Fourie is not the family's real name. They changed it when they relocated to South Africa. *David* isn't telling *Julie* his real identity," Lady Anthea said on her way to her bedroom.

"He's certainly acting as her protector. I see that parallel, but maybe he doesn't *know* his old family name," I offered. "I think Elvis is going to be more help getting us unstuck." Then I walked away with my song back to ear worming in my head. "A trap!" I held my banana aloft. "We need a trap," I called to her over my shoulder. "I'll be ready in ten."

* * * *

When we got to Buckingham's, Shelby was already hard at work. The three of us checked in the campers, boarders and dogs in need of grooming.

Mayor Betsy Rivard was in the early group, leaving Paris and Riley to stay overnight. "I'll be presiding at the commemoration festivities this afternoon and tonight, so I thought it best not to have to worry about running home to take these two out."

I smiled and thanked her. I was thinking about how I needed to contribute to the Lewes rumor mill and she'd be a good person to start with, but it wasn't the right time. She seemed to have more to say to me, though. "I wanted to thank you and Lady Anthea for testifying yesterday," she said.

"I don't think my statement got us very far," I said with a laugh. "All the credit goes to Lady Anthea."

"Your suggestion to use a 3-D facsimile was genius." She paused and looked around the lobby to be sure we were alone. "This extravaganza his organization has planned has so many aspects and contractors there would be no way we could pull it off without him on site. The man is truly a visionary and a force of nature. Wait until you see the afternoon educational events and tonight's entertainment. You'll be amazed!"

"I can't wait," I said.

"I don't know how he stays in business," she went on. "He personally kept up with every detail. I asked his administrative assistant if he was this hands-on with every project and she said she'd never seen him give as much special attention to a project as he had in Lewes."

"His son helped, didn't he?" I asked.

"He wasn't even expected to be here. Howard was surprised when he learned David would be joining him." She checked her phone and gasped. "Look at the time. I've *got* to run."

I waved goodbye and went back to my office and texted Rick. "Bring your wetsuit with you tonight."

"Sue, can we talk?" Dana stood in the doorway. She was holding her laptop. Mason and Joey were behind her.

I motioned them in and they lined up in front of my desk.

"I used HooRU on someone else," Dana said. "You had Julie Berger in the photo you took of the Fouries."

"What did you find? The suspense is killing me."

"That's just it, I didn't find anything."

"So, she's never done anything to get her photo in a newspaper or on the internet? Isn't that unusual for someone her age?" I asked.

"Never? Ever?" asked Mason, with loads of skepticism. "No social media? Yeah, it's unusual."

"No relatives that look a lot like her?" Joey asked.

"I didn't see a resemblance between her and Billy B., but with the age difference and him being her great-uncle, it didn't seem like a big deal," I said.

"Shelby told us she was trying to get into acting. How can there be no photographs of her on the internet?" Dana asked. "She hasn't gotten any parts?"

"I know of another source of information on her." I picked up my phone and dialed Chief Turner. "Have you finished reading the emails between Julie and Billy B.? I'm putting you on speaker."

"I'm doing it now. We thought we had something a half hour ago. She wrote to him about two brothers fighting in her kitchen and she had to throw a cup of water on them to break it up."

"The brothers were cats?" I asked.

"Yeah, how did you know?"

"Everybody knows that. Can I come over and look at them?" I asked.

"Be my guest," he said. "Pretty boring stuff. She was a first-grade schoolteacher for a year and now doesn't look like she does anything."

"I'm on my way."

* * * *

I thought I had read five hundred boring emails, but it was more like fifteen. *I finished James Patterson's latest Women's Murder Club book. My favorite so far.... The diner on the corner has the biggest desserts! ... Do you think I should paint my apartment light blue or...*

I threw my head back. "Yeah, I can see she's a real criminal mastermind. How can someone living in New York City, going on auditions, who looks the way she does have such a boring life?" I asked. "She's got to be editing here, picking and choosing what she wanted him to know."

"These emails may be boring to you, but they probably meant a lot to Billy B.," John said.

"Why did she say they spoke on the phone, instead of saying they emailed?" I asked.

"Maybe they did both. I don't have his landline phone records yet," John said, shaking his head.

"What about a background check on her?"

"Yes, if you call that a background," Chief Turner said. "It's more like no-man's-land."

"Do you know what that term means?" I asked.

"Uh, yeah, I do."

I told him anyway. "It's land left unoccupied because of fear. Maybe that describes her," I said. I thought about how Lady Anthea and I had speculated that they'd had sex after the dinner at Gate House, which was the day they met. "Well, there's a man now. It's David Fourie."

Chapter 33

We had allowed extra time to get to Billy B.'s "celebration of life" service. Parking spots were at a premium because of all the tourists in town for the commemoration events. Martin Ziegler and Julie Berger stood outside the door to Mozart's greeting everyone.

Lady Anthea took Julie's hand in hers. "I believe I hear Beethoven's 'Fidelio.'" Still holding the young woman's hand, she turned to Martin. "How thoughtful of you to play a German opera since I understand that's what Billy B. sang to your customers."

"Yeah. Howard Fourie picked it out," he said. Letting go of Julie's hand, she deftly walked off with Martin. She turned and motioned for me to keep up. "I'm an opera fan, but I also enjoy your Arthur Miller."

"*My* Arthur Miller? I don't have an employee by that name," Martin said. "You must be mistaken."

"Arthur Miller was an American playwright. He wrote *Death of a Salesman, All My Sons.*" She paused to see his reaction. "*The Man Who Had All the Luck?*"

Martin shook his head. "Nope, not ringing any bells."

I was still following them, wondering if there was a point to all this, when she lowered her voice and said, "He often used the relationship between fathers and sons as a theme. One character says, 'A child can never disappoint a father, but a father can disappoint a child.'"

"Excuse me." We stepped aside for Howard Fourie to get to the door. I was about to say good morning, but he kept walking. He seemed distracted and despondent.

Lady Anthea drilled a look into Martin's slowly comprehending face, before going on. "I believe you feel you've disappointed your son. That's why you continue with these shenanigans. You've been ratcheting up the crazy, so to speak, all this week. Rick loves you very much. He will always love you, but your actions affect him. Your actions are beginning to affect those that care about Rick. I would ask you to remember that."

"I want to make this right, but I don't know how," he said.

Lady Anthea turned around to me. "Sue?" Her tone suggested she'd served him up and the rest was up to me.

"If you know anything that can help Chief Turner find Billy B.'s murderer, you need to tell him today," I said.

"I've told him all I know," he said.

I looked away from him. He hadn't told us anything until he was confronted. "We'll see you inside," I said, and Lady Anthea and I walked into the deli. I leaned closer to her and whispered, "I wanted to get you away from him. You weren't going to tell him about our plans, were you?"

"Goodness, no," she said. She stopped walking and turned to me. "Do you think Howard Fourie could have changed his mind about Julie's suitability for his son?"

"I doubt it," I answered. "Why do you ask?"

"The overture he chose has to do with love being more important than freedom. I wondered if it was intentional."

The bistro tables had been moved to the sides of the small restaurant and chairs were lined up in rows in the middle of the room. A large photograph of Billy B. was on an easel in the front.

"Here comes Chief Turner," I said, in a desperate whisper. "Before he gets to us, just tell me something. Did it sound to you like Martin Ziegler just confessed?"

"What in the world do you mean? When?" Lady Anthea's eyes darted from one side of the room to the other, like she sensed danger galloping toward us but couldn't tell the direction.

"Just now! He said he wanted to make this right. What does he want to make right? What did he mean?" I asked, trying to keep the dread out of my voice.

John was closing in and he was smiling at me. I was getting more suspicious with every step he took.

"Let's talk about it later," she said.

"Did you see the look on Howard Fourie's face when he walked by us while you were talking to Martin? It was strange. He looked sad," I said.

Officer Statler came up behind Chief Turner and waylaid him. She said something that made his head jerk up to look at me. What had I done this time? Then he was walking toward me again, but without the smile.

Out of the corner of her mouth, like a really crappy ventriloquist, Lady Anthea said, "Incoming."

I nodded so she would know I'd heard her, then went to a safer subject. "I think if you are going to eavesdrop, you should practice so the eavesdrop-ee doesn't know you're listening."

"Who are you talking about? Us?"

"No, Howard Fourie," I said.

"Hello," John's baritone voice said. I wanted to ask what he meant by that but didn't want to sound paranoid or guilty, though I was both. "Can we speak outside?"

"Hello to you, too," I said. "They're about to start." I waved my arm in an arc in case he hadn't noticed the room full of people seated in rows of restaurant and folding chairs which faced the counter where Martin and Julie were standing.

He leaned close to the side of my face, almost touching my cheek, and I breathed him in. He whispered, "Martin Ziegler is coming in to confess."

Chapter 34

"There's only one reason Martin Ziegler would confess to murdering Billy B.," I said to Chief Turner, once we were on the sidewalk and away from any conduit to Lewes's rumor mill. I would need that network later, but not now. I had left Lady Anthea inside the deli at the service.

"Because he's guilty? I mean that's just a guess, but after almost two decades in law enforcement, I'm willing to go out on *that* particular limb."

Waves of soft, kind laughter reached us from inside Mozart's. I couldn't make out who was talking or what had been said, but the memorial service had begun.

I looked down and shook my head. "You can't possibly think he tried to break into my house last night!"

He took a deep breath and ran his hand over his head. "No. I don't see him putting in that much effort."

"Exactly," I said, looking him in the eye. "I think my intruder last night was the one who killed Billy B."

"Why did *you* think he wants to confess then?" John asked.

Louder voices came from Mozart's now.

"To Billy B.!"

"To Billy B.!"

I stood there looking at the crack in the sidewalk, not daring to look up because I was so afraid of what I was thinking. The only reason I could think of for Martin to confess to a crime —a serious crime—that he didn't commit was if he thought Rick did it, but why would he suspect his son? "No idea," I said. Our eyes met and we agreed he would accept my lie. The way we did that helped my conscience.

We heard chairs scrape and the general feeling of people moving around and talking. Opera started again. This song was different. I guessed German again, but it was only a guess.

"If he wants you there when he turns himself in, will you come?"

"Oh, you bet," I said, a little more schoolmarm-ish than I'd intended.

Chief Turner looked at the closed doors. They were made of glass, so the memorial service guests could watch us, if they wanted to. "Let's walk to the station. Officer Statler will bring Ziegler down."

"Look at all this traffic. You would think it was summer," I said.

"All right, I can take a hint. I won't say any more," he said.

"I wasn't just trying to change the subject. Traffic really is heavy with visitors coming to town for the high-tech display Mr. Edutainer and his son have planned for the commemoration events. A lot of the restaurants are going to be serving a dessert wine that's supposed to taste like the wine from the shipwreck," I said. "It's called Grand Constance. The winery made it in 2005, the year after the artifact was found, for their 320th anniversary."

"I know. I saw the application for the permit to sell it on the beach."

"You don't have to worry about public drunkenness. It's supposed to be so sweet and thick no one wants much of it." I knew I wouldn't be there to sample it, but still, it sounded like fun. "We even have a row of yachts in the bay, lined up," I rambled on. "Some sailed across the bay from Cape May, New Jersey, and others sailed in from the Atlantic Ocean!"

"Who's Mr. Edutaaaainer now?" He was laughing.

"Aw, do you think I'm entertaining?"

"You have no idea," he said.

I figured we were far enough away from the memorial service to laugh and not be inappropriate. We crossed the street at the end of the block.

"I want to set a trap for whoever really killed Billy B.," I said.

"I'm already not liking this." He stopped walking and turned to me. "If you don't believe the person that wants to confess is the real culprit, though everything points to him, then who do you suspect?"

"If I *knew* then I wouldn't need to use this elaborate con. And I would *tell* you." I explained to him all I knew about both Billy B. and the Fourie family's connection to Cologne, Germany, and about the HooRU app and how Dana had learned about the Nazi grandfather. Then I told him about Howard Fourie wanting his son to become head of South Africa's UNESCO commission, and my suspicion about the timing of Billy B.'s murder. "It had to be before David got to town." He listened without interrupting me and I liked that.

We were walking again. "I'll bring him in for questioning," he said, making it sound simple, but still unpleasant. "Want to know why I don't think Howard Fourie murdered someone I doubt he even knew existed? And by the way, most murders are committed by someone known to the victim. They hardly traveled in the same circles. If Billy B. had this information on the Fourie family, he could have told the world—not just David—and at any time during the weeks Fourie has been here in Lewes."

"Maybe he felt it would be worse to look bad in his son's eyes than in the eyes of the world?"

Then he exhaled. "He's going to lawyer up so fast."

"There's more," I said.

"Of course there is."

"What about Julie Berger?" I asked.

"I'll admit, she always gets a convenient case of shyness or grief or whatever, before she can be questioned," he said.

I told him about her asking David to take her with him when he left. "And there's Sandy Westlake," I added.

"That boat captain? When Billy B. was killed he was taking us to the Harbor of Refuge Lighthouse on Monday, remember?" he said.

"He could be involved in some way, right?" I was grasping at straws. "Was he the one who reported the incident at Irish Eyes yesterday?"

"He tried to make it anonymous, but, yes, it was from his cell phone and he was at Mozart's when he placed the call," John said.

"He tried to steal Wags and I made him put the dog down," I said.

"You just told me more than I got out of anybody that was at Irish Eyes yesterday. It was like a convention of blind, deaf people. Nobody saw anything. Nobody heard anything."

"So now that you know what kind of person he is, don't you think you should question him about the murder?"

"I get that for you attempted dognapping is as serious as murder, but it's not for me."

"We know that Captain Westlake and Martin wanted to use Wags for breeding. He and Billy B. could have gotten in a fight over the dog. So those are my three suspects. Really Lady Anthea's and mine, and you have Martin Ziegler," I said.

"Why don't I just arrest the whole town?" he asked.

"The way I see it, you don't have to *prove* anyone *guilty*. You just have to keep them from leaving town."

"What did you have in mind?" he asked.

"If there was a rumor going around town that evidence that would solve the case had been found, he or she might try to get it," I continued.

"Rumor? I can't be a part of disseminating misinformation," he said.

"You don't have to," I said. "We'll take care of that."

"That sounds like something from one of those books you like to read, but tell me more. Where is this imaginary evidence?"

"Not in a public place, but not too private either," I said. "Some place the killer would have to make a real effort to get to." I stopped to gauge his reaction, but he was his usual stoic self. Then I thought about how he'd taken me in his arms last night. He wasn't stoic then. "I want people to think it's at the Harbor of Refuge Lighthouse."

He opened the door to the city administration building and we walked through to the Lewes Police Department offices. It seemed ages ago that I had been sitting on that sofa with Lady Anthea and Rick. He led me to the same interview room.

"I've seen way too much of this room lately."

"Did you use that facial recognition app on me?" he asked.

"What? No! I wouldn't do that."

He didn't respond, instead he asked, "Will you be okay waiting in here while I telephone the Coast Guard about tonight?"

I went in and sat down, which he interpreted as me being okay. He was still talking. "They can use their personnel and facilities to assist federal, state, and local agencies and I believe their assets are especially suited for whatever is going to happen tonight. So do you mind waiting in here?"

I was indoors; the room was stuffy; my friends were eating Mozart's food. Hell, yeah, I minded. I just hadn't had the heart to say so. Chief Turner was telling the Coast Guard about our amateurish, Elvis-inspired, half-assed scheme. I grabbed my cell phone and called one of the few people I wanted to talk to at that moment. I hadn't told Lady Anthea where I was going and I'd left her at the memorial service without a ride back to Buckingham's for the agility class. The call went directly to voice mail.

"It's Sue," I whispered, afraid Chief Turner would be back any minute. "I'm at the police station." I told her about Martin's plan to confess and what I thought his real reason was. I was about to launch into why Rick couldn't, wouldn't, didn't kill Billy B. when the door opened and I quickly hung up, hoping she'd check her messages soon.

John came in, followed by Officer Statler and Martin, who was startled to see me.

"I don't need her here!" he said. Was he firing me? Could I be evicted if he didn't want me here?

"Why not?" John asked.

"She hassles my friends," he said, leaning his back against the wall.

"Like Sandy Westlake?" I asked.

"Well, yeah."

"He tried to steal Wags again," I pointed out.

"What's the big deal?"

"Are you kidding me?" I couldn't believe my ears.

Martin looked at Chief Turner, who was standing by the door. "If someone wanted to kidnap you to go have sex, would it be the worst thing in the world? I ask you."

"Actually, yeah," John said. "I wouldn't like it. It would be illegal."

"Why are you trying to confess to a murder you didn't commit?" If I was about to be thrown out, I wanted to do as much damage to his plan as I could, as quickly as I could. "Why do you think Rick killed Billy B.?"

Chief Turner's head, and that of Officer Statler, jerked from me to Martin, then back again. I'd jumped ahead a few squares. They'd have to catch up.

"He certainly didn't!" I yelled.

Martin wilted into a chair and put his head in his hand. When he looked up he asked, "Can I talk to her by myself?"

Chief Turner looked at me. "You good with that?"

I nodded and got up and moved to the chair next to Martin. I put my hand on his back.

"Let's go," Chief Turner said to Officer Statler. He reached for the door.

Martin watched the door to be sure it was fully closed. "I didn't find my car at *your* house!"

"But the traffic camera showed you driving it!" I countered.

"Yeah, on Savannah Road." He had me there. Chief Turner had said the cameras along the street photographed him.

"Where did you find it?" I asked.

He didn't answer, so I stayed completely still. Which I happen to be good at. I imagined myself sitting on my surfboard.

Finally he said, "In front of Raw-k & Roll."

"How did you know to go there?" I asked.

"I knew Billy B. wanted dog food, so when the car wasn't at Buckingham's, I went to another place where somebody could steal dog food from. I figured he wouldn't try to break in to a big pet store. He wouldn't know how."

"So you didn't follow the fumes and smoke to my house?" I asked.

"Nah, I don't know where you live," he said. "Well, now I do since it was in the paper. Plus when I was in here on Tuesday you said something about my car being at your house."

I had been keeping my eyes glued on Martin to pick up if he wandered into that place where he thought he could make up anything he wanted and pass it off as his own truth. Now I glanced up at the ceiling. He was right, I had revealed the part about my house in that interview. I wondered who else had seen that article in the paper. Last night's visitor?

"Shelby saw your, uh, very unique car, at my house. So how did it get to Raw-k & Roll?" I asked.

He didn't answer. Looked like he had no intention of telling me, so I answered my own question. "The other night we were wondering how the killer got away after he killed Billy B., and we just assumed it was on foot. Now we know the killer drove your car. And now I get why you couldn't answer Chief Turner when he asked if Billy B. was alive when you retrieved your car from my driveway. You were never at my house." I took a deep breath and revised my opinion of the man sitting next to me. "On Monday when Chief Turner was trying to identify the body and Rick couldn't reach you, he thought it might be you. That you might be dead. He was devastated," I said. I let that lean on him a few seconds then picked up again. "So, you see, Rick didn't kill Billy B. He didn't even know he was dead. What you've done today is a completely unselfish act. That's very rare. I think you're a good father."

"Keep that to yourself," he said.

I looked at Martin. His eyes had teared up, and he tried to hide a sniffle.

"Are you pretending?" I asked.

"Yeah, you got me. It's a thing I do."

Chapter 35

Martin Ziegler told John about the car being left at Raw-k & Roll after I hastily constructed and negotiated an immunity deal for him.

After Martin left, I said, "Now that we know Billy B. didn't steal dog food from Rick, I'm wondering if he came to my house *to return* what he stole from Buckingham's?"

He smiled indulgently, making it obvious what he thought of my excessive faith in my fellow man.

"Wouldn't that make more sense than a serial dog food thief?" I asked, in my defense.

"Yeah, I guess it would," he said with a laugh. "Since he printed those articles of you and the Pet Place—"

"Pet Palace."

"Whatever. It was the night before the break-in, which means it was planned. Why would he regret it so soon after he stole your merchandise?"

"It was so unlike him, or what I've learned about him," I said.

"We may never know the why," he said. "I've got to see if there's anything useable in that car." He smiled and walked me out.

Now I had to find Lady Anthea and get us back to Buckingham's. Her phone was turned off, or she was screening my calls. She hadn't checked in with Shelby either.

"Where are you?" I asked her when she finally called me back. "Why are you whispering?"

"I'm in Julie Berger's hotel room," she said.

"What are you doing there?"

"I came back here with her after the memorial service to talk to her. She was telling me that the UNESCO presidency was Howard Fourie's

dream, not David's. Then David came and now she's outside with him."
She was talking fast.

"Can you hear anything they're saying?"

"No, she closed the door."

"Good! If the door's closed, look through her stuff," I said.

"I can't go through her personal belongings," she said. "I've been looking through what she's left about, but I can't find anything that contradicts what she's told us about who she is. Wait, I need to see if she's coming back in. I'll look around the curtain." A few seconds later, she called out, "Steady on!"

"What's happening?"

"He's proposing marriage!"

"How can you tell if you can't hear them?" I asked.

"He's down on one knee!" she said. "Julie's about to cry. He's taking her hand." The play-by-play continued. "He's placing a seashell on her finger where an engagement ring should go. Now he's putting it in her hand."

Lady Anthea had stopped her running commentary and the suspense was killing me. "What's happening now?"

"Julie said yes and they're kissing."

"I'll get the car and pick you up. She'll be outside for a while so look around while you wait for me," I said.

"Sue, do you think they knew one another before this week?" Lady Anthea asked. I was startled by the thought, but their relationship had progressed at greyhound speed. "Oh, my! Could *she* be coming here? She is!"

"Who is? What's happening?" Her tone had me yelling for more information. I got in my Jeep and started driving to Savannah Road.

"Officer Statler is here. She's talking to Julie. I'm going out there," Lady Anthea said.

I heard the police officer saying, "Ms. Berger, I need for you to come with me to the station. We need to discuss issues surrounding your uncle's murder."

The officer's words sounded canned; she had probably rehearsed it on the way over. So John thought Julie might be less likely to get upset if her interview was conducted by another woman. I guessed it was worth a try. And I doubted many police chiefs were this patient through a fainting spell, the crying, and the postponing of the interviews because she was too upset. The truth was she had information he needed. She might be able to connect Billy B. to Howard and David Fourie.

"Don't let her get upset!" I yelled to Lady Anthea. I hoped I hadn't been put on speaker.

Julie was saying, "Really? Right now? I have to do this now?" That was followed by a couple of huffs.

I heard David say, "Can't this wait?" If the three of them were leaving the country right after the evening event, no, it couldn't.

"No, it cannot wait," Officer Statler said. "My car is parked at the curb. Let's go."

Then Lady Anthea said, "I want to accompany her!"

"No, ma'am. I can't allow that," Officer Statler said.

Lady Anthea stammered in confusion.

I heard Julie say, "David, find me an attorney!" Why did she feel she needed an attorney? I wanted her to testify now more than ever.

"A lawyer?" He was confused, too.

"Yes!"

"I will!" he promised. "Don't worry!" He didn't need to know why. Surely unconditional love like that was rare. Or maybe it was all around and I was blind to it.

I drove as far as Front Street but then the volume of cars on their way to the library, the museum or the ferry terminal made it impossible for me to do more than inch along.

"Will she let you ride in the car with Julie if you commit a crime?" I asked.

"I wouldn't advise that," Officer Statler said. So I was on speaker. Great. She'd heard what I said but she hadn't said it *wouldn't* work.

"Commit a crime!" That was the best suggestion I could come up with, and that tells a lot about the state I was in.

"I stole this handbag," Lady Anthea said.

"Uh, ma'am, I believe that's your own handbag."

"I was about to steal that man's wallet!" Lady Anthea yelled.

"He's practically inviting you to!" Officer Statler yelled. "He's turning around and pointing to the pocket it's in."

"Let her go with me!" Julie yelled.

It was official. They were all yelling. I hung up.

When I crossed over Savannah Road, I was in front of the hotel. Julie was getting into the backseat of the police car. I turned into the packed parking lot and waited for Lady Anthea to see me. She was about to get in behind Julie. We made eye contact and she nodded toward David. Then she followed Julie into the cruiser. I guessed that was a first. When I pulled up to where David stood, I saw he was madly swishing the screen of his phone.

I lowered the window and called to him. "Get in. Let's go." Traffic in the opposite direction was moving at the speed limit. The backup was only on the way to the three o'clock events.

He looked up and seemed startled to see me there. "Uh, Sue Patrick?"

"Yes, get in. We'll follow them to the police station." That would give us time to talk. "You can count on Lady Anthea to stand up for her interests."

"I have to find an attorney for Julie." His voice softened around the name. "She thinks she needs one. Can you help me?"

I still wanted to ask if he knew why she felt she needed a lawyer but stopped myself. A murder had more than one victim. If, in its wake, we suspected our neighbors, friends, or lovers, we were victimized, too. Sure, much less severely, but we still lost. If I planted a seed of doubt in David's mind, he and Julie would be casualties. His attitude told me he didn't care why she felt she needed an attorney. Good for him.

"Of course," I said.

While he walked around the vehicle and climbed in, I was racking my brain to think of an attorney. Had Rick found someone for his father? I meant, a real lawyer. The law wasn't the occupation of any of my surfing friends. The very thought made me snort and I had to cover it up with a cough. Surely someone among all the pet parents in town practiced law. There was one person I knew who was retired now, but had practiced law in Delaware. He had been a district attorney, supposedly a good one. Did I dare get the person I had in mind involved? I never voluntarily entered his orbit. Hadn't David's day gone to hell already?

I pressed the necessary squares on my dash to place a call. "Call Charles Andrews."

He answered on the second ring. "Ms. Patrick? Is So-Long all right? He better be!"

David turned to me in confusion and I smiled weakly at him. "Charles, I'm with someone whose—"

"My fiancée, it's my fiancée who needs an attorney. She has been taken to the police station."

"What's her name?"

"Julie Berger."

"And yours, young man?"

"I'm David Fourie."

"I'm on my way."

What had just happened? Was he playing some kind of a trick? Would he even show up?

When we arrived at the police station, I told David I would park and then wait outside for Charles Andrews. David jumped out before I was at a complete stop.

I signaled to pull away from the curb and a driver honked his horn at me. Charles Andrews stopped the green Buick in front of me, illegally double parking. How had he gotten here so fast? What had I done? I stared as he spryly jumped out of his car and, moving faster than I had ever seen him go, he sprang up the pavement to the door. He was wearing a cardigan and had a briefcase under one arm. He tried to clip a bowtie to his collar but gave up after a couple of tries and a few choice words, and threw it on the grass. Now that he was the real Charles Andrews again, I felt free to drive off to find a parking spot.

As I walked up the sidewalk, I saw Lady Anthea coming out of the police station doors and called to her.

"Charles Andrews was magnificent," she said.

I indicated where I was parked and we went back to the Jeep.

"I was *invited* to leave when he arrived. Not that I could have stayed much longer." She pointed to her wristwatch.

"Were you able to keep her calm enough for the interview to start?" I asked.

"For it to start, yes. Chief Turner told her that they had opened Billy B.'s safe and he showed her his will. It said everything had been left to her. Then Mr. Andrews came in and introduced himself as her solicitor. That seemed to relax her." We got in the Jeep and she continued, "I was thinking about what Julie said about the UNESCO position not being David's dream."

I told her about how he'd been during the drive to the police station. "I really think all he cares about is doing what's best for her."

"Yet, when he's in public or with his father he certainly acts like the UNESCO promotion is what he wants," she said.

"Elvis once said—"

"Oh, no."

I began again. "Elvis once said, "There's the image and then there's the man.""

* * * *

On the drive Lady Anthea told me about the food served at the memorial service. She had dined on Austrian potato salad, red cabbage, Viennese beef goulash, and venison bratwurst. We made it back to Buckingham's with just enough time to go over our plans for the afternoon and evening one more time before the agility class began.

Dana would start the rumor at Cape Henlopen High School and we expected an uptick in disciples when the parents found out.

"Dana's part-time modeling helped get her hired at the last minute for the afternoon event at the library," Shelby told Lady Anthea. "She'll tell a few people there about something being found on the lighthouse."

"She's underage. Is it fair to ask this of her?" Lady Anthea said, massaging her temples.

"Dana wouldn't have it any other way!" Shelby said. "After the murder is solved, she wants to put this on her college admissions applications."

"After Henry's murder we sat down as a group and talked about this. Granted, we may have been a little generous, since we were working under the assumption that there wouldn't be another murder in Lewes in our lifetime. Fair is fair and we did agree we would do everything we could to be sure she was safe, but we would never lie to her or treat her like a kid," I said.

* * * *

Since Lady Anthea had an agility class to teach, she would have to miss the three o'clock start of the Virtual Reality History Lesson. In three venues visitors could interact with our fantasy forerunners and at each we would be there hinting that the police had a lead in solving Billy B.'s murder. Police officers would be going to the Harbor of Refuge Lighthouse at daybreak. "How exciting," we would imply. Then we would let Lewes's rumor machine take over from there. We wouldn't lie. The Buckingham Pet Palace didn't get its sterling reputation by being dishonest. We would hint and we would keep complete deniability.

"I'll go to the library," I said. This landmark building in downtown Lewes on Adams Avenue was the newest Lewes attraction.

"I'll take Zwaanendael Museum," Mason said. That venue was built in 1931 to commemorate the 1631 Dutch settlers, the first European colony.

"I've got the ferry terminal," Shelby said. "Joey will stay here. Then Dana and he will come with us to the beach event at six o'clock."

I looked around the lobby to be sure all the pet parents were outside with Lady Anthea and not able to hear us, then turned to Mason. "Were you able to get everything we'll need?"

He nodded. "Everyone has stepped up."

* * * *

Dana stood at the main entrance to the library, dressed as a seventeenth-century maiden and handing out virtual reality glasses, in exchange for your driver's license. I was one of a group of ten people arriving around the same time. As Dana handed us our glasses, she recited her lines, "Lewes was discovered by Henry Hudson as he traveled up the Delaware River in the summer of 1609. The town was settled by the Dutch in 1631. Enjoy your afternoon learning about this historic seaport, Lewes, Delaware, through projected animations and virtual reality characters." She stepped aside for us to enter. Then she looked surprised. "Chief Turner, I didn't expect to see you here. After, well, you know—"

I turned to see him behind me looking confused. He glanced around to be sure she was talking to him. Since he's the only Chief Turner, or Chief Anything Else, in town, that was a no-brainer. How long would it take him to catch on? One thousand one. One thousand two.

"I mean, what they found on the lighthouse." Dana was playing her part to perfection, except for the fact that she hadn't mentioned the murder. She could have been talking about finding anything on the Harbor of Refuge Lighthouse, from osprey droppings to a lighthouse keeper's old boxer shorts.

Chief Turner strode past us and went into the library, in a pretend huff. "Can't discuss an ongoing murder investigation," he grumbled. "Sorry."

He didn't speak to me, but I saw the corner of his mouth fighting a grin. I took the virtual reality glasses from Dana and gave her a wink.

At various points inside the library we were instructed to put on our virtual reality glasses. Additional virtual characters in the library would tell about the Dutch surrendering the land to the British, and continue to 1682 when the territory was given to William Penn, and the town was named Lewes, after the town by the same name in Sussex County, England, though it was part of Pennsylvania. At the same time, in the Zwaanendael Museum, virtual men, like Colonel David Hall of the Continental Army, gave eerily lifelike talks about the American Revolution, and other eighteenth-century happenings, such as the sinking of the *Severn* in 1774. At the Cape May–Lewes ferry terminal, nineteenth-century virtual reality people explained the bombardment of Lewes in the War of 1812. Buckingham spies at each had started texting me.

"Whoa." I stepped back at what, or rather who, was standing in front of me.

"The area known today as Lewes, Delaware, hosted many notorious pirates, like me, Captain Kidd. Arr, arr, arr," the tall virtual pirate said.

"Arr, arr, arr," a baritone voice close behind me said.

I yanked off the glasses to see Chief Turner. He was walking away and I followed him to a section of nonfiction books. I wanted to know what he'd learned from Julie Berger. Maybe we wouldn't need our plan after all, but somehow I couldn't see that being the case.

A ping told me a text had come in on my phone. I pulled it out of the pocket of my khakis, hoping Chief Turner wouldn't turn around until we got wherever he was leading us, which was the biography section, if I wasn't mistaken.

The text was from Joey, and had been sent to Mason, Dana, Shelby, and me.

Having a hard time getting clothes for Lady A. Says no to everything. Btw, what the hell are trainers? She won't wear them.

Dana: *Kicks.*

I typed, *What are kicks? Maybe a windbreaker and slacks for her?*

Mason: *Athletic shoes. Recommend what Sue said and walking shoes. Like Mephisto. Sue will pay for them.*

We went radio silent. I had a picture of Lady Anthea on the back of a Jet Ski, in February, at night, in her wool pantsuit and sensible pumps. Maybe even a strand of pearls.

"Sue?" My brain registered that it wasn't the first time he had called my name.

"So I have you to thank for Charles Andrews's appearance?" he asked.

"Sorry about that. How did it go?"

"I think I gave her more information than she gave me," he said.

"What else was in the safe other than the will?"

"Old newspaper clippings. I think some were from when he was a kid."

"Can I look at them?" I didn't have much time but I thought it might be important since Julie hadn't ruled herself out as a suspect.

"I have someone over there if you want to go now," he said.

I thanked him. I knew the only reason I was getting that undeserved okay was because he was busy with the crowds drawn to Lewes by the celebration and frustrated by his inability to get useful information from his two suspects.

"I heard back from the Coast Guard. They're set up on their end. I'll be in touch when it's all over."

I thanked him in some vague way and we headed back to the library entrance. "I'll admit it. I'm impressed. This is really first-rate," I said.

He nodded in agreement and walked away.

When I got in the Jeep, I was checking for a new text from Joey when what Chief Turner said hit me. And it was like that proverbial ton of bricks. He would be in touch when it was all over? I looked around for his police car. It was parked in the row facing mine, down a couple of spots, and he was in it.

I jumped out and made my way through the throngs of people waiting to get into the library. The line wasn't one person behind another. In Lewes we were always talking to each other, so our queues were three- and four-deep batches of friends, even if we had met for the first time in that procession.

By the time I got to John's car, he was pulling out.

"Stop!" I yelled, standing in front of the car, waving my arms.

He rolled down the window and I walked around to talk to him.

"What's the matter? What happened?" he called, the concern in his voice apparent.

"It was what you said!"

"What?"

"About letting me know when it's all over. I'll be on the lighthouse tonight, waiting for whoever shows up," I said.

"I'll be following whoever comes out there and I'll signal the Coast Guard," he said. "Let's keep it simple."

"It's too late for that," I said, and turned to walk back to my car. My plan wasn't simple. Was it my fault if he had that impression because I had only told him one part of it? Well, yeah.

He pulled back into his parking space. The lot was crowded and he was lucky no one had taken it. By the time I was in my Jeep his long legs had brought him to my window.

"What are you saying?" He didn't wait for me to answer. "You started the rumor that we found evidence on the lighthouse. That's all you have to do."

I shook my head. "I'll be on the lighthouse waiting for whoever takes the bait and shows up. I thought you'd be there, too."

"There's no need for that. I'll stop whoever it is—and I think it will be Martin Ziegler—before he gets to the lighthouse." I watched him walk off. He wasn't stomping away. He was almost strolling. He thought he had won.

"You have no idea how large the bay is, do you?" I yelled to his back. I detected a slight slowing of his pace. "*Welcome to My World,*" I said. Partly because I figured an Elvis reference would annoy him, but also because that's what the ocean, seventy percent of the planet, was.

Chapter 36

I was fuming, but that didn't stop me from going to Billy B.'s condo. I was barely back to Savannah Road when my cell phone rang. It was John.

"You really didn't use that facial app on me?" he asked.

"I really didn't. You can tell me what you want me to know about where you came from and whatever else," I said.

"California," he said.

"Where in California?"

"Hollywood."

"Lord," I said.

"Anything else you want to know?"

"Uh, are you really a police chief or do you just play one on TV?"

He laughed. "I'm for real."

"When it comes to your relationship with your father, are you more like Rick and Martin Ziegler or like Howard and David Fourie?"

"I don't have a relationship with him. I was ten years old the last time I saw him." He sounded matter of fact, but I could hear the undertones of an old, scarred-over hurt. "He was my mother's third husband and when they split up he divorced both of us."

"You seemed to have turned out great, so his loss." I was wishing we weren't having this conversation over the phone, but he had started it. "Are you close to your mother?"

"I guess. For years her acting career was pretty much dormant, but in the last few years she's gotten a lot more roles. I think the reason for those lean years was because she refused to consider grandmother roles. Now that she's playing those parts she's working again."

"I'm at Plantations East, so I better hang up. Was this a peace offering?" I asked.

"Maybe. Did it work?" he asked.

"No, I'm sorry. I'm still going to the lighthouse."

"I've got to get to work," he grumbled.

"Thanks for telling me…" I said, but he had hung up.

The young officer was photographing the yellowed old papers from the safe. He logged each and put it in a plastic bag. I introduced myself, and he said that Chief Turner had alerted him that I was on my way. I sat and read through the plastic. Some were the quality of high school newspapers back in the day of the typewriter. Most were dated in the early 1940s and the photographs were black and white. Once I found the commonality, it was obvious.

When I got back in the Jeep, I telephoned Chief Turner. I was guarded and he was stiff, but I told him my theory. "I think I know why she never wanted to come in for questioning. Most of her family was killed in the Holocaust—always by someone working for the government and wearing a uniform. Billy B. and his brother, her grandfather, were just kids, but they inherited this fear of anyone in a uniform. I believe it was passed down to her, too."

"You were able to learn all that from those papers?" he asked.

"And from what Julie told me. Historical trauma is real. And I think that's what she suffers from."

* * * *

Shelby and all the part-time hostesses were at Buckingham's by five o'clock. I staffed the desk while she met with them in my office. It was crowded, but the information she was giving them was important. I saw movement near the floor. It was Abby trying to squeeze out of the room and she was looking at me between lots of legs. I went over to rescue her. When I had her safely out, I picked her up. She weighed forty pounds but I wanted to hold her for a minute. I kissed the side of her face and put her down. She would stay with Shelby.

All the boarding dogs would get personal attention when the fireworks started at six o'clock. The dogs would share rooms so each Buckingham hostess could cuddle two at a time.

The sun would set at five-thirty, and the laser lightshow with narration would start then. Classical music would be played in the background.

The local radio station would broadcast the audio for anyone not willing to tolerate the volume of traffic that had been nonstop since yesterday morning. The tales of the 1774 storm and later sinking of the *Severn* in Roosevelt Inlet, with the 2004 dredging of Lewes Beach which scattered many artifacts on that beach, including the wine bottle section from South Africa, would be offered to those listeners, everyone standing or sitting on Lewes Beach, and over the loudspeaker at Buckingham's. Shelby would turn the radio off when the fireworks began.

She and our group of part-timers filed out of the office. I thanked them for working the extra hours and told them I'd see them later.

"I'll go home and change now," I said, walking around the reception desk. Lady Anthea was already there waiting.

"The doors will be locked after seven. You'll need a special password to get back in," Shelby said, grinning.

"What is it?" I asked.

"I'll text it to everybody." She was already typing on her phone. "Sue," she called to me, coming around the desk. "Be careful!" Then she hugged me.

"I will."

Chapter 37

I walked the short distance to my house. The Jeep was parked on the driveway since I had already hitched the personal watercraft trailer on to it and loaded the Jet Ski.

Lady Anthea was sitting on the sofa, talking into her computer tablet. She liked to Skype home when she was here. I stayed out of her way and went to my bedroom to change into my wetsuit. She had been adamant that she would not wear one. She had agreed to the slacks, windbreaker, and walking shoes compromise.

When I came out, she stared. "That's why I refused to wear one of those," she said.

"Why?"

"Because I wouldn't look like you. That's why."

"As long as your body does what you need it to do, what does it matter?"

I took two plastic sandwich bags out of a drawer and handed one to Lady Anthea. "For your phone."

She took it and walked over to her handbag on the coffee table. Was she planning to take her handbag on a Jet Ski?

"Are you okay doing this?" She could be thinking about last night and not wanting to stay home alone. "You're welcome to stay with Dayle on the beach. She'll be keeping an eye on the Fouries. That should include Julie Berger, but in case it doesn't, you could follow her," I suggested. We assumed they would stay for all the congratulations at the finale, but wanted eyes on them.

"No, I'd rather go to the lighthouse," she said.

I nodded. "That settles that. Everything okay at home?" I asked, pointing to the tablet.

"I had an inexplicable desire to talk to my brother," she said. It wasn't inexplicable to me, but I didn't comment on her word choice. Just the fact that she had called him was quite the exposé on the state of her nerves. She had wanted to talk to family.

I looked at my watch. "Shelby came up with a password we'll need to get back into Buckingham's after seven." I read it to her from my phone, "*Did Elvis regret the cape?*"

Lady Anthea gave a nervous laugh.

"It's five-thirty," I said. "Time to go."

* * * *

We took back roads to Cape Henlopen State Park, both to avoid traffic and being seen.

"Oh, no," Lady Anthea said when she saw the park was closed for the night.

"I have a friend in the park service who's going to let us in." When we were near the guard shack a young woman in the tan park service uniform came out and lifted the arm to the gate and we drove through. She never looked at us.

"She wasn't very friendly," Lady Anthea said.

"She didn't see us, and we didn't see her," I said. "The park closes at sunset."

We made a left at the fork, then another left, then a right turn for the two-mile drive north to The Point where we would launch the Jet Ski.

We parked in the parking lot and I began unhooking the trailer so we could get the PWC to the water.

"Is this where you and your friends come to surf?" she asked.

"We do come to Cape Henlopen, but not this part of the park. We surf at Herring Point. It's not surfing like they do in California or Hawaii, but we have a good time," I said.

The Harbor of Refuge Lighthouse and Delaware breakwater looked close enough to touch, but that was an illusion. The so-called sparkplug-style lighthouse also looked the size of a sparkplug, when it was actually seventy-six feet high. I pointed to our left. "We're at the mouth of the Delaware Bay." Then to the right. "That's the Atlantic Ocean." The Point extended north between the two. The breakwater where the lighthouse sat ran northwest before crooking off west. The Harbor of Refuge Lighthouse sat on the southern end, which made our trip a lot shorter. The breakwater was a mile and a half long.

"I see the yachts that came to watch the commemoration ceremony," she said, pointing further up the bay.

My phone lit up with a text from Dayle. I read through the plastic bag, *"Can't find Martin."*

I didn't want to think about the effect that bit of news was going to have on Rick.

I handed Lady Anthea a life vest, then I texted Mason, Rick, Dayle, Shelby, and Dana. *Underway.*

Mason's cryptic reply came next. *In position.*

Chapter 38

I slid my hand through the safety lanyard and pulled it tight around my wrist. The whistle on the end dangled. I had no intention of being thrown from the watercraft. I helped Lady Anthea onto the Jet Ski and then I climbed on in front of her. I clipped the lanyard to the stop button, pressed the go button. And slowly pulled away.

When we were in open water I accelerated. Lady Anthea hadn't spoken since she'd thanked me for the life vest.

The night sky was clear and my mood lifted. Soon we were nearing the breakwater and I slowed. This was the outer breakwater. Some people, like Charles Andrews, still called it the new breakwater. We went from one side to the other, checking for movement or even a flashlight, before I pulled up to the side of the dock. I pulled a line out of the storage boot and then reached for the railing of the dock. I used a clove hitch knot to secure the Jet Ski. I got out and then helped Lady Anthea onto the dock. I pulled a tarp out of the hold and covered the PWC, then slung my backpack over my shoulder. "Let's go."

We walked the length of the dock and climbed the stairs up to the lighthouse. Staying out of the light, we leaned up against the cast-iron structure. I imagined some of the lighthouse's steadiness seeping into my body.

"Thank you," Lady Anthea said.

"For what?"

"For another adventure," she answered.

Waves broke over the stones of the breakwater. Some of the stones were the size of a car.

"You're welcome," I said. "I've been meaning to ask you something. Remember, when we were talking on the phone on Monday and you said you needed to tell me something. You said that you didn't know how it came about. What was it?"

"My brother wants to come with me on my next visit," she said.

"The duke?" I asked, not knowing how I should feel about the prospect.

"Yes, but he'll probably forget he ever thought of it."

I checked my phone for texts. There was a group text from Dayle and I read it to her. "The Fouries & Julie here on beach."

What about Martin? I texted back.

He was looking for someone to complain about the wine to. Wants a refund.

Then I heard the sound of a motor. A boat was on its way to us. "Then who is that?" I whispered.

We watched as it pulled up to the dock. Captain Sandy Westlake crawled out.

"Sue Patrick, I know you're here."

Chapter 39

I pressed my cell phone into Lady Anthea's hand. "Stay," I said.

"I'm not a dog," she said.

"I meant, stay here in case I get in trouble."

"How will I know?" she asked.

"If I sound funny. I don't know. You just will. I've got to go."

Before she could argue or ask any more questions, I walked forward. The lights from the forty-foot boat were still on and I came out of hiding and confronted him from one bright pool. "I'm right here." I walked down the steps from the lighthouse base to the dock.

"Funny thing. I've lived here since I was born and worked on the water my entire adult life. Never thought I would ever be on a lighthouse. This is the third time I've been on this lighthouse in a week." Captain Sandy talked in a lazy, drawn-out tone.

The dock was cantilevered to the breakwater to make it more resilient to the force of the waves. Sandy Westlake and I faced each other and swayed a little.

"When was the first time? When you brought Wags out here?" I asked. I had no idea what he was talking about, but figured I would play along.

"Yeah, when I heard how much he was worth, I wanted to breed him. Billy B. thought someone else stole the dog, and that I could help him get it back." He laughed. "So I let him go on thinking that."

"Who did he think had the dog?" I asked.

Captain Sandy chuckled again, but didn't answer. Instead he said, "He stole some dog food to try to bargain with. He was going to leave town after he got the dog back."

So he was afraid of someone, I thought. That's when I heard the sound of a Jet Ski, or some brand of personal watercraft. At first I thought it was mine being stolen and that Lady Anthea and I were about to be stranded on the Harbor of Refuge Lighthouse. I saw a light over Sandy Westlake's shoulder. The craft was getting closer.

Sandy turned to watch as it tied up. Chief Turner climbed onto the dock. I watched Sandy's face to see his reaction to the police showing up. Was the guy crazy? Instead of the fear I expected, he looked relaxed. I turned to see John's expression when he saw me standing on the dock in my wetsuit.

"He's stalling for time. I don't know why," I said to him.

John stared at him and waited. Even in the dark, I saw the spring-loaded tension of a predator. Not many people could hold out with that level of intensity, but obviously Sandy Westlake was made of sterner or stupider stuff.

"Chief Turner isn't really interested in dognapping. What did you have to do with Billy B.'s murder?" I asked.

Westlake's eyes widened at that, but he didn't say anything else.

I looked at John. "Billy B. was afraid of someone in town and Sandy knows who it was." I turned back to our neighborhood dognapper and would-be breeder. "I think you're stalling for time. I want to know why."

He chortled and looked out into the water. The only change was that this time I detected a nervous laugh. And he had gazed at the water. He was looking for something, or someone. I pushed. "Tell us who Billy B. was afraid of, or else you'll regret it." A large wave rolled under the dock and when we swayed, my voice wobbled. I hoped he hadn't noticed. "Or else," I repeated, going for a stronger-sounding tone, one that "brooked no argument," as *The Felonious French Friends* author had written.

I heard a roar coming from behind me and turned to see Lady Anthea. She flung herself at Westlake knocking him off the dock. He fell, arms and legs flailing into the two-hundred-twenty-feet-deep ocean. She turned around and smiled at Chief Turner and me, and wiped her hands together. She was proud of herself.

Chapter 40

John leapt to the side of the dock to help the sputtering, spitting man. I realized I could be shocked later, but now I needed to help. We each took an arm and pulled. Sandy Westlake leveraged his legs against the posts of the dock and we were able to lift him up and out of the frigid water.

When we got him on a sort of terra firma, I turned to Lady Anthea. "Why did you do that?"

"Because you said, 'or else' twice." She looked at him with disgust. "He looks like the kind of person who could cut up rough."

John did a double take, then turned to Sandy Westlake. "I'm arresting you for the murder of…"

"Murder! Wait a minute! I didn't murder anybody," he said, beginning to shiver.

"I believe you were an accessory…" John continued.

"I want an attorney," he said.

"Doesn't everybody?" I asked. "So, did Billy B. think he was seeing Howard Fourie's father when he saw Howard for the first time? Is that what scared him enough to leave a town he'd lived in for years and loved?"

He stuck his bottom lip out and glared at me.

John was on his radio calling for someone.

"Listen," I said to John. "Do you hear that?"

In the moonlight I saw a dingy boat heading for the group of yachts. Then as I watched, it veered off to the largest yacht, which was anchored south of the others.

Sandy Westlake smiled.

"That's Howard Fourie?" I asked him.

He nodded and smirked. The guy was really childish. "I get paid if he makes it to his yacht."

John turned to jump on his Jet Ski. "I don't think the Coast Guard can get there in time."

"Wait," I yelled.

Then I hit speed dial. "Do you see him?" I asked Mason.

"Sure do," he said.

"I've got to go," John yelled.

I put him on speakerphone. "Waaait. Waaait," we heard Mason say to our friends. Then he said, "Now!"

One after another they stood up on their paddle boards. Then they shook the inflatable Pugs, which had been filled with Mason's iridescent recipe. Soon, the bay was scattered with the Pug ghost dogs. Wags had his revenge. To get to his yacht, Howard Fourie would have to go through them. The small boat with a small motor turned starboard, then to port. The engine stalled out. Behind it, a Coast Guard vessel approached. On a loudspeaker, we heard the captain identify himself and order Howard Fourie to stop and allow— "What the hell?" the captain yelled when he saw the Pugs.

Chapter 41

Buckingham's opens at nine o'clock on Saturdays so I slept until seven. After my beach run, I treated myself to a smoothie at Nectar. I was about to pay when I heard a deep voice behind me.

"This is on me," John said.

I turned to him and smiled.

"And on them," he continued and pointed to a big table in the back dining room.

I looked and saw Rick, Dayle, Martin, Jerry, Charlie, Lady Anthea along with our entire staff and ran back to them with arms open wide. "I don't understand. How did you all know I was coming here?"

"We had good intelligence that you were walking this way," Mason said, pointing at John. "But if you hadn't come in here, we would have scrambled to go wherever you went."

Shelby stood and raised her juice glass. "Sue, we will always scramble to go wherever you are."

I choked back tears because I needed to get something out. "I was so worried about all of you on those paddleboards last night."

"That's a trick I taught her," Martin Ziegler said, when he saw I was about to cry.

I walked around the table thanking each for the role he or she had played in bringing Billy B.'s killer to justice. Then I ordered pancakes. I sat next to John and we talked about what had happened through the night as he had questioned Howard Fourie.

Fourie knew that Rick was Martin's son. After he killed Billy B., he took the car to Raw-k & Roll, broke in, stole enough dog food ingredients to make it look legit, and left the car there. He thought of that at the last minute, to confuse us, and it had. Fourie wanted Billy B. out of the way before David arrived—and he was coming to Lewes on Monday.

"He knew David would never become the president of his country's UNESCO commission if it came out who his grandfather was," Lady Anthea said. "UNESCO is the United Nations Educational, Scientific and Cultural Organization. They must be above reproach."

"He seemed more upset about that than getting arrested for murder," John said. "Lady Anthea, he mentioned something he heard you say about an Arthur Miller play."

I lowered my voice so Martin, at the other end of the table, wouldn't be able to hear me. "That explains the look on his face when he overheard you talking to Martin."

She smiled and changed the subject. "These large *pommes frites* are excellent." She was pointing with a French fry.

"Who tried to break in to Sue's Thursday night?" Joey asked.

"That was Captain Westlake. He's under arrest, too. It was part of his deal with Howard Fourie," John explained.

John put his arm over the back of my chair. "Now you've got them all thinking they can solve crimes?"

I just shrugged and laughed. What had I started?

He leaned closer and almost in a whisper, asked, "Sue, what do you want me to do about Martin stealing Wags from Billy B.? You don't want people going around stealing expensive animals, I'm sure."

"How would you feel if your last memory of a friend was doing something like that to him? Can we let the crime be the punishment?"

"Okay," he said.

Over John's shoulder I saw Julie Berger and David Fourie walking along the sidewalk, his arm around her waist, their heads close. He held Ariadne's leash with his other hand.

John looked to see what I was staring at. "Things are going to be tough for that kid." He sounded sympathetic and I smiled.

"Do you think he'll be terribly disappointed not becoming the South African UNESCO commission president?" Lady Anthea asked.

I shook my head. "Julie said it was never his dream."

"What is his dream?" John asked.

"She is." Then I went back to my pancakes. "Can they make it as a couple?" I asked. "Lady Anthea, did that opera have a happy ending?"

"Let me just say that *Ariadne auf Naxos* has one of the most difficult to sing arias in all of opera. It does have a nice ending, but it takes a lot of hard work."

John looked at me and then back at Julie and David. They had stopped and he had cupped her face in his hands. They kissed. "Looks like they're going to try."

"His father killed her uncle and his grandfather killed *so* many people." I turned back around to the table.

John was looking at me, waiting.

"So this," I said, pointing to myself and then to him, "could be '*T-R-O-U-B-L-E.*'"

Meet the Author

Lane Stone, husband Larry Korb, and the real Abby live in Alexandria, Virginia, during the week and Lewes, Delaware, on the weekend. When not writing, Lane is enjoying characteristic baby boomer pursuits: traveling and volunteering. Her volunteer work includes media and communications for the Delaware River & Bay Lighthouse Foundation. She's on Georgia State University's Political Science Department Advisory Board. She serves as College/University Coordinator for the American Association of University Women for Virginia and on Northern Virginia Community College's Women's Center External Advisory Board. She is currently pursuing her post-graduate certificate in Antiquities Theft and Art Crime. Her alma mater is Georgia State University. Her standard schnauzer, Abby, tweets as TheMenopauseDog. You can find Lane at www.LaneStoneBooks.com.

Stay Calm and Collie On

Don't miss the first book of the Pet Palace Mysteries series!

Buckingham Pet Palace is known for treating dogs like royalty—until murder dethrones its good reputation!

As owner of an upscale doggy daycare and spa, animal-lover Sue Patrick pampers pooches for the most elite clients in Lewes, Delaware. Surely she can survive a weeklong visit from Lady Anthea Fitzwalter, her well-to-do business partner from England. But before Sue can serve her guest a spot of tea, she discovers more-than-a-spot of blood inside the company van—and all over the driver's dead body . . .

Someone abandoned the van full of dogs at the Lewes ferry terminal and got away with murder, leaving Sue and Lady Anthea pawing for clues. With a fundraising gala approaching and Buckingham Pet Palace facing scandal, can two very different women work together to fetch the culprit from a list of dodgy suspects—or are they heading toward a proper disaster?

Chapter 1

"Sue! Hi!" My customer gave the Buckingham Pet Palace lobby a furtive once-over. "Is *she* here?"

No need to say who *she* was.

I propped my elbows on the reception counter and lowered my voice like I was about to reveal news to her and her alone, secrets people would kill for. "Her flight from Heathrow landed on time. She flew into Dulles. The driver called me from there and then again when they crossed the Bay Bridge." I was happy to indulge her curiosity with minute details; after all, I had worked long and hard to get everyone in Lewes, Delaware talking about Lady Anthea Fitzwalter. The whole town seemed to be looking forward to the first visit of our very own royal personage.

"Good afternoon, Lydia." My head groomer, Mason, joined us, leading a geriatric beagle. He handed our customer the leash, then pivoted to give me a tired, put-upon nod.

"Thanks for fitting us in. I wanted Loopy to look his best for Friday's gala."

Mason turned back to her and managed a weak smile. I telepathically dared him to point out that the beagle looked pretty much the same after a groom as before, the exception being the Union Jack bandana Loopy now wore. Though only in his mid-twenties, Mason was one of the best dog groomers in Delaware. This particular dog had hardly been a challenge, still I complimented him on a job well done. But received no acknowledgment.

"You look tired," she cooed. Bingo! That's what Mason was longing to hear.

"Exhausted. You have no idea." Mason reached a toned and heavily tattooed arm down to give Loopy one final behind-the-ear scratch, then dragged himself away, calling over his shoulder, "I did teeth and glands."

She turned back to me. "Sue, is he okay?"

"He's loving every minute of it." Mason's hangdog expression hadn't fooled me at all. He tells me weekly that he's an artist. On Saturday he told me he was suffering for his art. I slid Lydia's credit card slip across the counter and showed her where to sign. "Both of my groomers are booked solid getting all the dogs ready for the gala." Abby, my standard Schnauzer, still needed to be groomed. It was only Monday, so I wasn't worried. I discreetely tucked the receipt into a cellophane bag along with a gluten-free dog treat in the shape of a blow-dryer.

She patted her shoulder bag. "I have my invitation right here. Engraved, even. Oh, my. Very nice." She paused in her quick sentences. "Might we see Lady Fitzwalter during the week here?"

"Oh, yes. She'll be in and out all week. Drop by anytime for tea." I pointed to the table of Twinings tea and Wedgwood mugs, which we have out every day. Our usual fare of Walkers shortbread had been replaced by the more labor-intensive clotted cream and scones. Of course, the Savannah Road Bake Shop had done the heavy lifting in baking the pastries. I'd purchased the clotted cream from a British specialty grocer in Wilmington. Though Walkers sported the coat of arms and the words, *By Appointment HM the Queen*, showing their Royal Warrant status, I wanted something special for my co-owner's visit.

Our contract allowed Buckingham Pet Palace to use her likeness and her name, but Lady Anthea had gone above and beyond that with her frequent emails, sometimes asking astute business questions, sometimes attaching photos for me to use. I appreciated all she'd done to make the Pet Palace a success and I wanted her to know it.

The front door opened and my afternoon receptionist floated in. Dana would be starting her senior year at Cape Henlopen High School next month. She has the biggest afro in the history of the world. My blond hair is cut short, so balance was maintained in the hair universe.

"Hi, Dana," Lydia and I said at the same time.

"Hey!" She and her hair leaned over to pet Loopy. She's truly beautiful—not pretty, not attractive—but beautiful. She takes advantage of our relative proximity to Manhattan to model part-time. I wondered how many hours she would be able to work at Buckingham's in the fall and how much time she'd spend in New York, beefing up her college fund.

Loopy lay down and rolled over on his back. A blatant appeal for a belly rub from Dana. Lydia shook her head. "None of that, young man. They have a party to put on," she said, giving the leash a slight tug. The dog reluctantly accepted defeat and stood. "See you Friday," she called on their way out.

"Bye. Don't forget to come back any afternoon for tea," I called.

Then I turned to Dana. "Am I ever glad to see you! It's been crazy here."

She came around to join me behind the desk. "And it's only Monday." She looked at the dashboard document on the computer screen. "Looks like we have double the number of dogs in day camp than usual!" She checked to be sure the lobby was empty, then she broke into a little dance. "Yay us!"

I had to laugh. "The schedule is like that all week." I took a deep breath and looked longingly at my office. It's along the back wall, as is the reception desk, but tucked behind a wall. When I was at my desk, I could see and be seen by the staff, but not by pet parents on the other side of the counter. On said desk there was a to-do list I'd pummeled into submission. I rubbed my forehead and tried not to think about the amount of money I'd spent making Lady Anthea Fitzwalter's first visit to Buckingham's a success. Her week-long stay, topped off with the Pet Parent Appreciation Gala, should give us financial stability, assuming any small business could ever have that. With all the new day camp and boarding clients, not to mention grooming appointments, my gamble was paying off.

I turned back to Dana. "We just have to keep our heads above water this week and we'll be fine. I'll be in my office. Yell if you need me."

I made a beeline to my computer to check the status on the few arrangements yet to be finalized. There was an email from Beach Blooms with a photo attached. For the gala, they had initially proposed gardenia topiaries to delineate the space on the beach and gardenia plants for centerpieces, but gardenias were toxic to dogs. What did they have for me this time?

How about yellow orchids and coral roses to mirror the sunset? The photograph was of a sample on the beach at Roosevelt Inlet, at sunset.

Perfect! I wrote back.

All of the gala arrangements had fallen into place just like that. The Event Request Form had been approved almost before the ink was dry. The Noise Amplification Form had been signed overnight by the mayor and city council.

I kicked my sandals off and put my feet up on my desk. I laced my fingers behind my head and sighed. I don't know about you, but when my nails were done and my house was clean, I felt like I could do anything. Only one of these was the case, but that's the feeling I had. Like I could rule the world. Of course, my house was clean. Lady Anthea had asked if she could stay with me. My cottage-style house in a new section of town was cozy but modest, whereas the Inn at Canal Square, in historic downtown Lewes, was old-world elegant. It's very expensive, but each of their seven rooms was decorated with antiques. Who wouldn't prefer that? Lady Anthea, that's who. Her own house had a name, it was Frithsden. Mine did too. It was *house*.

The walls in what we called our Sleepover Suites were decorated with photographs of the estate that she'd provided. There was one for each season. Our customer restroom had framed photos of the Frithsden gardens that looked natural and free, but at the same time planned, a feat only the English could pull off. Those images I'd lifted from the internet. Downton Abbey has nothing on Frithsden. Then there was the revelation, thanks to Wikipedia, that we had been mispronouncing the name of her estate for over a year. It wasn't Fri*th*sden, like we'd been saying, it was Friz-den. For about a month we'd all walked around repeating it, over and over, so we wouldn't slip up when we met Lady Anthea in person. Obviously, she was used to something better than my spare bedroom, but she emailed that if I had a guest room, and that if it wouldn't be too much of an imposition, that'd be A-OK with her. Actually, "brilliant" had been her word. She'd said she would enjoy getting to know me better. Truth be told, it was a lot more convenient for me. My house was in the residential area behind Buckingham's and in easy walking distance.

At five o'clock on the dot, pet parents flooded into the lobby. I could hear Dana checking out day campers. Shelby, my assistant manager, had joined her and was checking in overnight boarders.

The main phone line rang. "Buckingham Pet Palace, this is Sue Patrick."

"This is Kate Carter, Robber's mom," the voice on the other end of the line said. The eyes of her female collie mix were circled with dark brown fur, making her look like she was wearing a mask. Robber was a regular at day camp and always used our door-to-door service. Lewes was a beach town but not everyone here was on vacation. We're happy to pick a dog up from his home. For a fee, of course. I've heard of pet spas in California that use limousines. Show-offs. We're happy with a Honda van painted our signature golf-course-green with our logo. "Could you tell me what time she'll be brought home?" Kate asked.

"Henry left at the regular time. He was dropping off four dogs. Would you hold while I check to see where he is now?" I left my office and headed for the reception desk. "Shelby, have you heard from Henry?" Then I noticed she had a phone to her ear.

Shelby had been my first hire. She was forty-five, about five years older than me, and five-foot nothing. With that red hair, she may not be tall, but you wouldn't call her short. She shook her head, no, then put the phone under her chin. "It's Mr. Andrews. So-Long isn't home. He says he absolutely *must* eat at five sharp." Shelby's eyes betrayed just a hint of a roll, nothing the customers in line would notice. Then she pointed to Dana, who was on a call herself.

"Paris isn't home either," Dana stage-whispered, her shiny hair swaying. "I have Mrs. Rivard on the phone."

"I'll call Henry." I pulled my cell phone out of my pocket and speed-dialed his work cell phone. While it rang, I whispered for Dana and Shelby to tell Kate Carter, Charles Andrews, and Betsy Rivard we'd call them back. After a generous number of rings, the call went to voice mail. I knew he'd see the missed call and didn't bother to leave a message. "He's not answering. Maybe he's walking a dog in now."

The three of us took care of the remaining ten clients in line.

"Who was the fourth dog in the van?" I asked.

Shelby searched in her curly hair for her glasses, finally extricating them. "Dottie, that Dalmatian puppy, was with them. We haven't heard from Dayle Thomas. She's the pet photographer, right?" She reached over and dialed the phone.

"Yeah, I'll try Henry's cell again." No answer. Enough of hoping he'd see the missed call. "Call me, Henry!" I told his voice mail. I walked around the counter and looked out the front window. Shelby had reached Dayle Thomas, and I went back to the reception desk to get the latest update.

"Ms. Thomas says Dottie is there. She had just gotten home from her photo shoot when Henry got there."

Dana moved closer to me to whisper, "Where is she?" She motioned to the large photograph of Lady Anthea Fitzwalter seated on what looked like an antique bench, ankles crossed, and flanked by two of her corgis. She was the centerpiece of the painting, but the bottom half of an ornately framed portrait of one of her ancestors could be seen over her shoulders.

"She's at my house." I dialed my van driver again. Nothing. "She's freshening up." Why did I just say that? I hate it. It implies you were something else before. All I know is, it's a phrase you don't want to overthink.

The bay window of our gift shop gave a better view of the side parking lot, empty except for my Jeep and Shelby's Prius.

Shelby raised an eyebrow. "She's probably running up your phone bill, making international phone calls to her idiot brother, the duke." There was a lull with no clients, so Shelby could speak loud enough for me to hear from the store where I was straightening a row of tiara chew toys. We *may* have Googled Lady Anthea's brother. We may have done it a lot.

Dana giggled. "That's harsh."

"Can either of you explain to me how he can make the same speech at every charity event and museum opening he goes to, and still not speak in complete sentences?" Shelby taught high school English until she had quit in a blaze of glory. She and her husband, who had been an analyst on Wall Street, visited our ocean one Christmas break and they never went back. She took a job walking dogs and realized she liked their personalities better than those of the children she'd been teaching.

"When Lady Anthea gets here, remember that we know nothing about her brother."

The phone rang and I was back in reception in a flash. Shelby covered the receiver with her palm. "It's chief somebody. He needs to talk to you."

"Huh?" I cocked my head from one side to the other, the way Abby does when she hears something she wants to understand but can't quite make out.

Shelby shrugged her shoulders. She didn't know who it was either.

"Is it something you can handle?"

She looked around to be sure there were no pet parents in the lobby and answered. Then she put the call on speaker. "This is Shelby Ryan. Can I…."

There was a roar over the line. "I AM CHIEF JOHN TURNER OF THE LEWES POLICE DEPARTMENT!" The man took a breath and I could hear dogs barking in the background. I had a visceral reaction to the distress I heard. "Your van was found abandoned in a line of cars leading to the Cape May-Lewes Ferry terminal parking lot. I am two seconds away from having the door forcibly removed."

"No!"

"No!"

"No!"

"No!"

Math's never been my strong suit, but there were three of us and four no's. I glanced up at Dana and Shelby. Their mouths were in O's and they were fixated on something over my right shoulder. Slowly I turned.

"Lady Anthea?" I reached my hand out to shake hers.

This was our first in-person meeting. I knew from her bio that she was about my age. And, like the picture in my head, she wore a knee-length skirt with a blazer. These were blue, accessorized by the Hermès scarf tied around her neck along with sensible pumps. Her eyes swept over the three of us dressed in khaki Bermuda shorts and green tops with Buckingham's logo. We were wearing our polo shirts, our summer uniform. In the fall we'd switch to button-down oxford shirts. I wasn't prepared for the raised eyebrow, nor the mouth in a hard, straight line.

Whatever. I ran to my office for my handbag—which is really a beach bag—and grabbed the keys on the plastic peg shaped like a dog's tail. I yelled at the phone, "I'm on my way. I'll be there in five." It would take me ten minutes. I motioned for Shelby to disconnect the call. "Shelby, call the DRBA police desk in the ferry terminal. Ask for Wayne. Tell him I'll buy him a drink if he stops this. Dana, keep trying Henry's cell."

As I ran by Anthea, it occurred to me that she might be able to help. What's the use of having a local celebrity if they can't get you and your dogs out of a jam? Without slowing down, I grabbed her arm. "Come with me."

Printed in the United States
by Baker & Taylor Publisher Services